GRONK™

a monster's story

volume 3

a comic by katie cook
colors for the interior pages by
kevin minor & eleanor schmitt

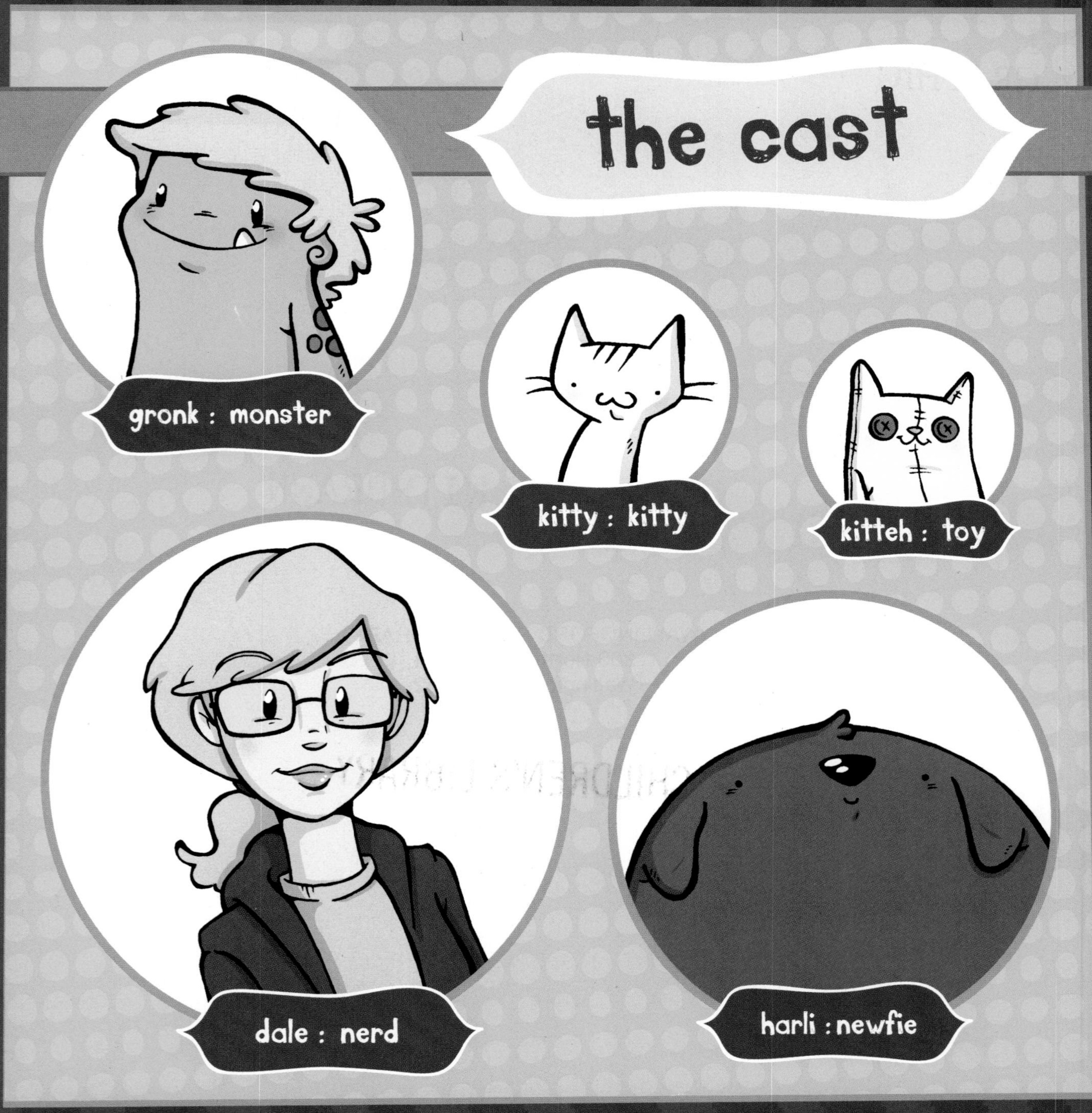
the cast
gronk : monster
kitty : kitty
kitteh : toy
dale : nerd
harli : newfie

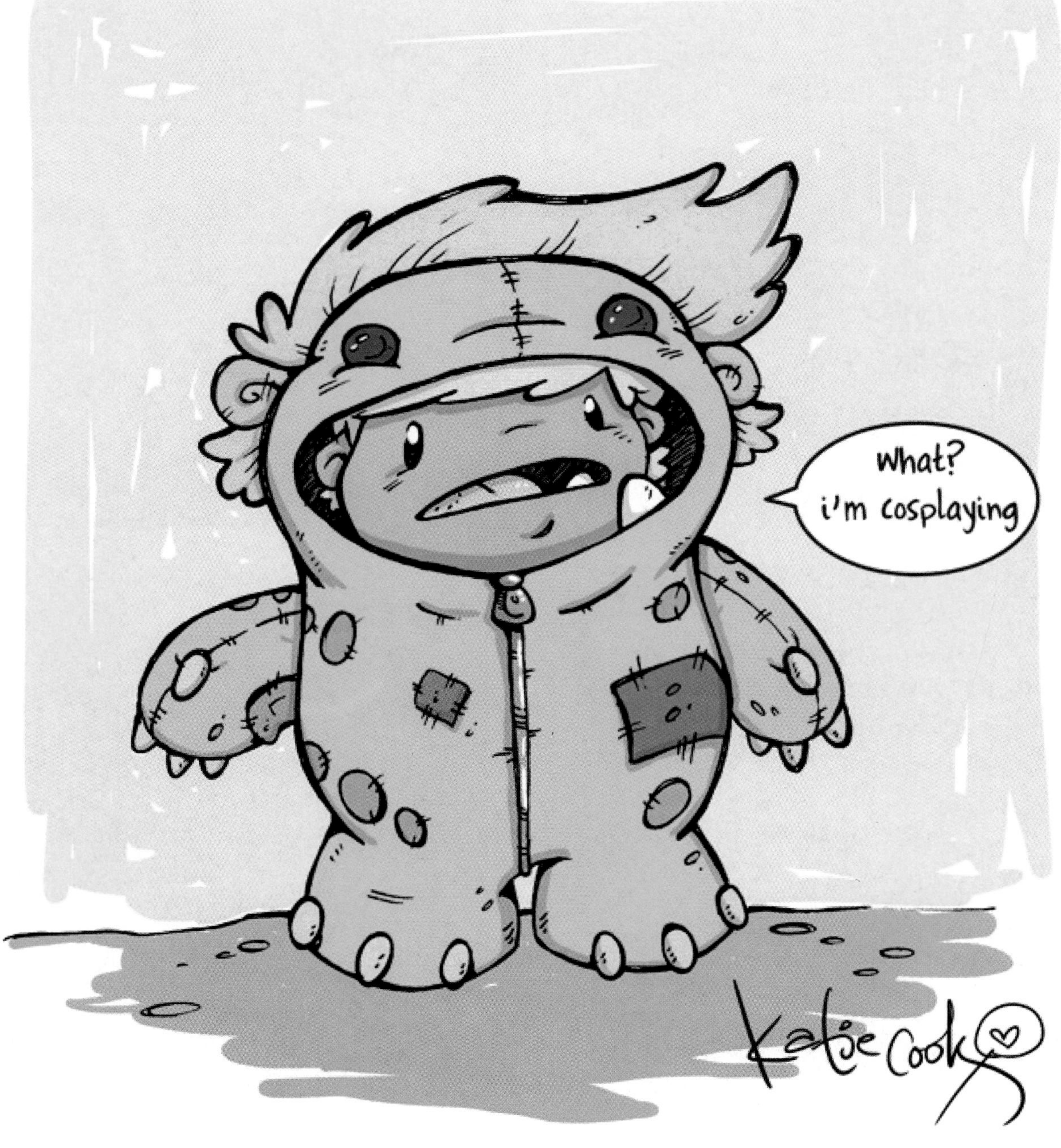
what?
i'm cosplaying
katie cook

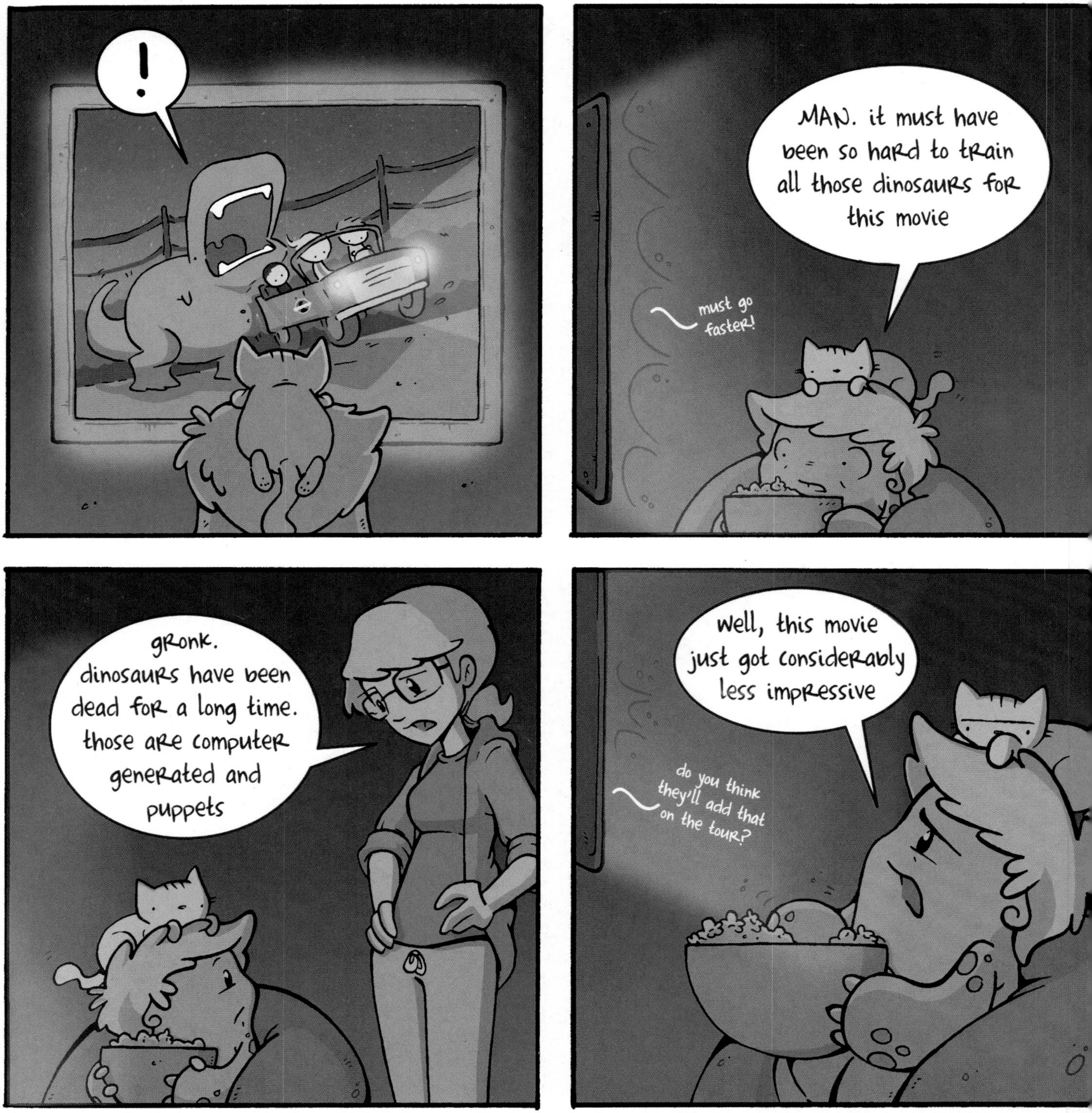
!
MAN. it must have been so hard to train all those dinosaurs for this movie
must go faster!
gronk. dinosaurs have been dead for a long time. those are computer generated and puppets
well, this movie just got considerably less impressive
do you think they'll add that on the tour?

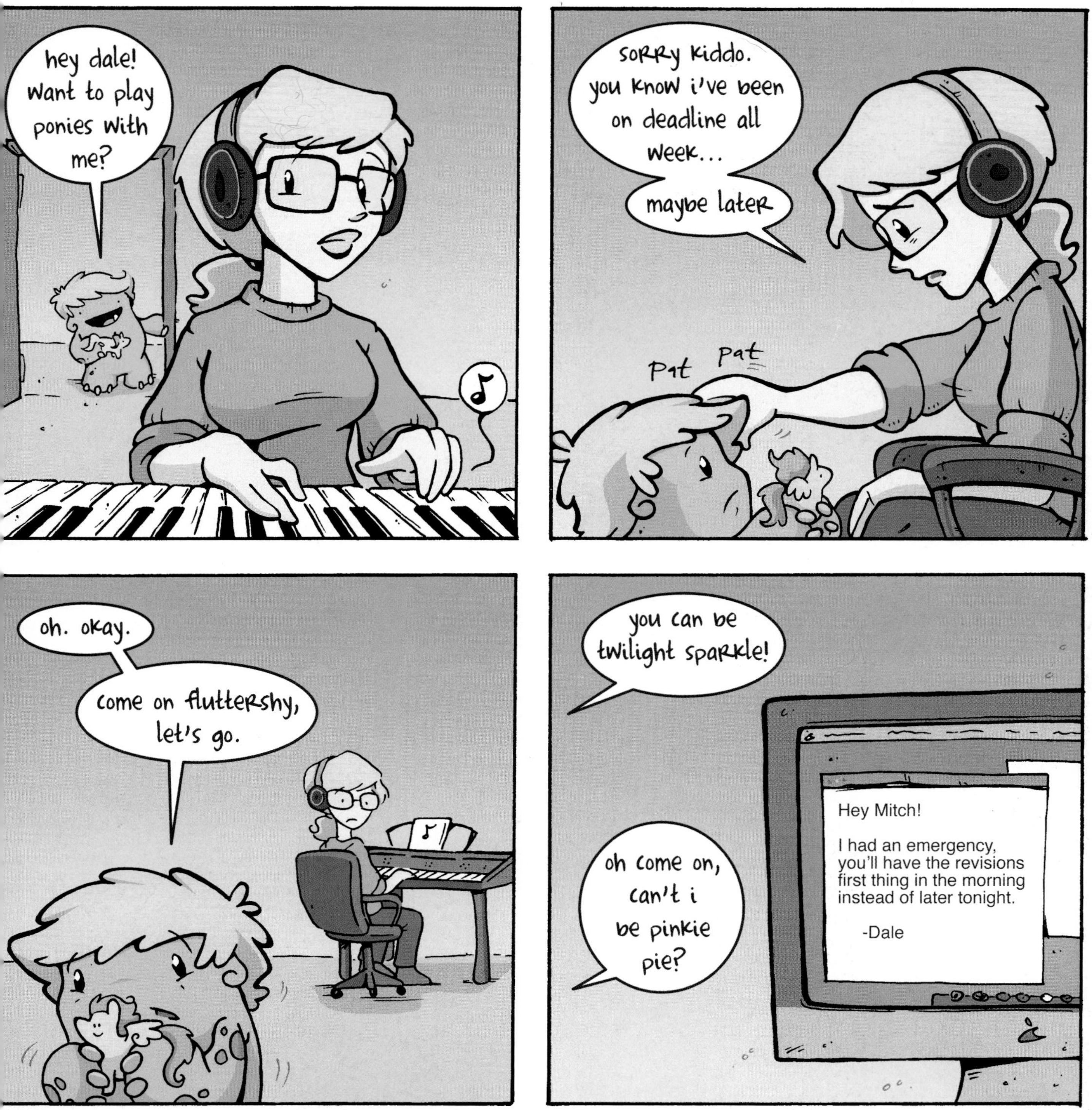
hey dale! want to play ponies with me?
sorry kiddo. you know i've been on deadline all week...
maybe later
Pat
Pat
oh. okay.
come on fluttershy, let's go.
you can be twilight sparkle!
oh come on, can't i be pinkie pie?
Hey Mitch!
I had an emergency, you'll have the revisions first thing in the morning instead of later tonight.
-Dale

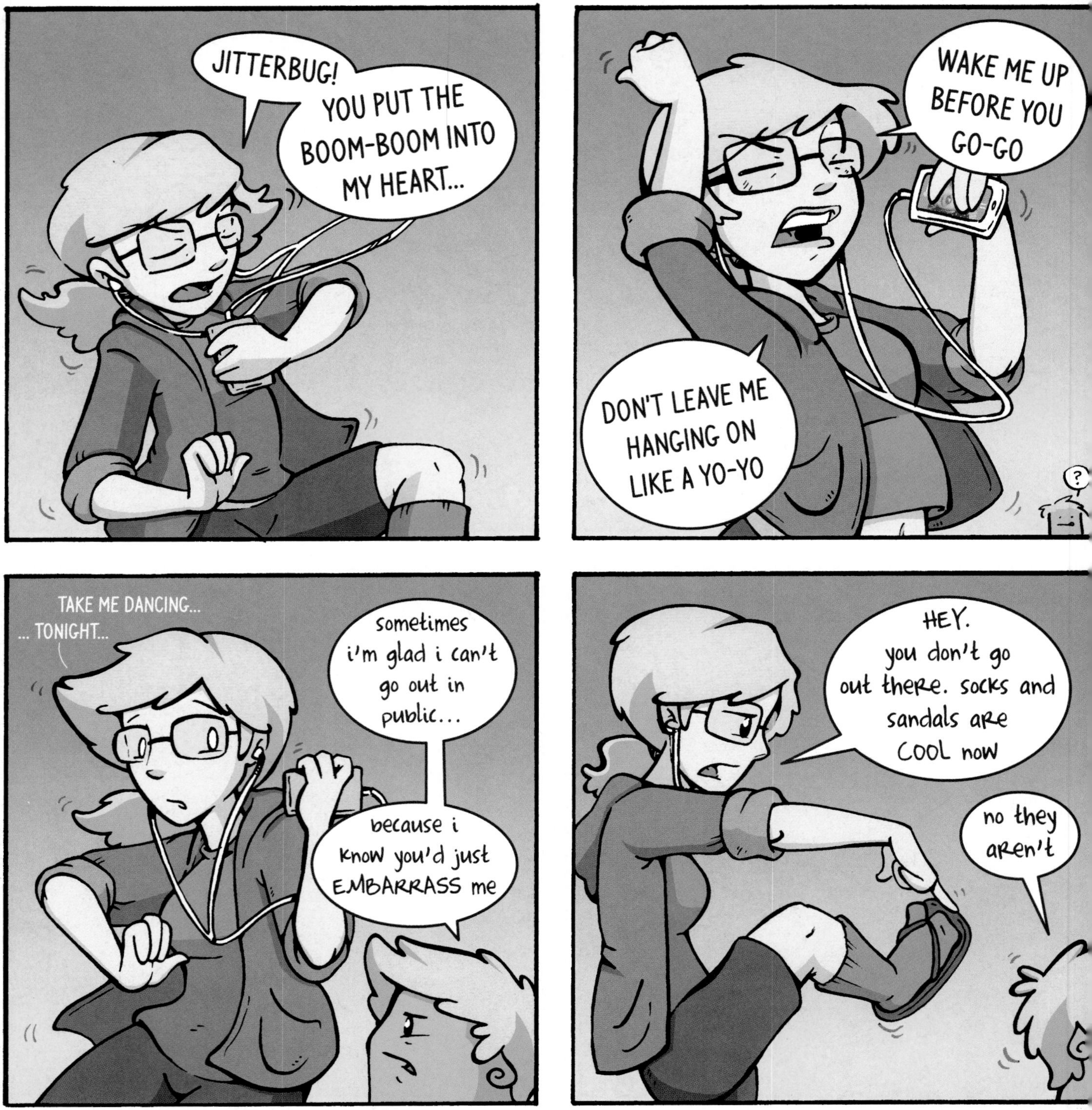
JITTERBUG!
YOU PUT THE BOOM-BOOM INTO MY HEART...
WAKE ME UP BEFORE YOU GO-GO
DON'T LEAVE ME HANGING ON LIKE A YO-YO
?
TAKE ME DANCING... ... TONIGHT...
sometimes i'm glad i can't go out in public...
because i know you'd just EMBARRASS me
HEY. you don't go out there. socks and sandals are COOL now
no they aren't

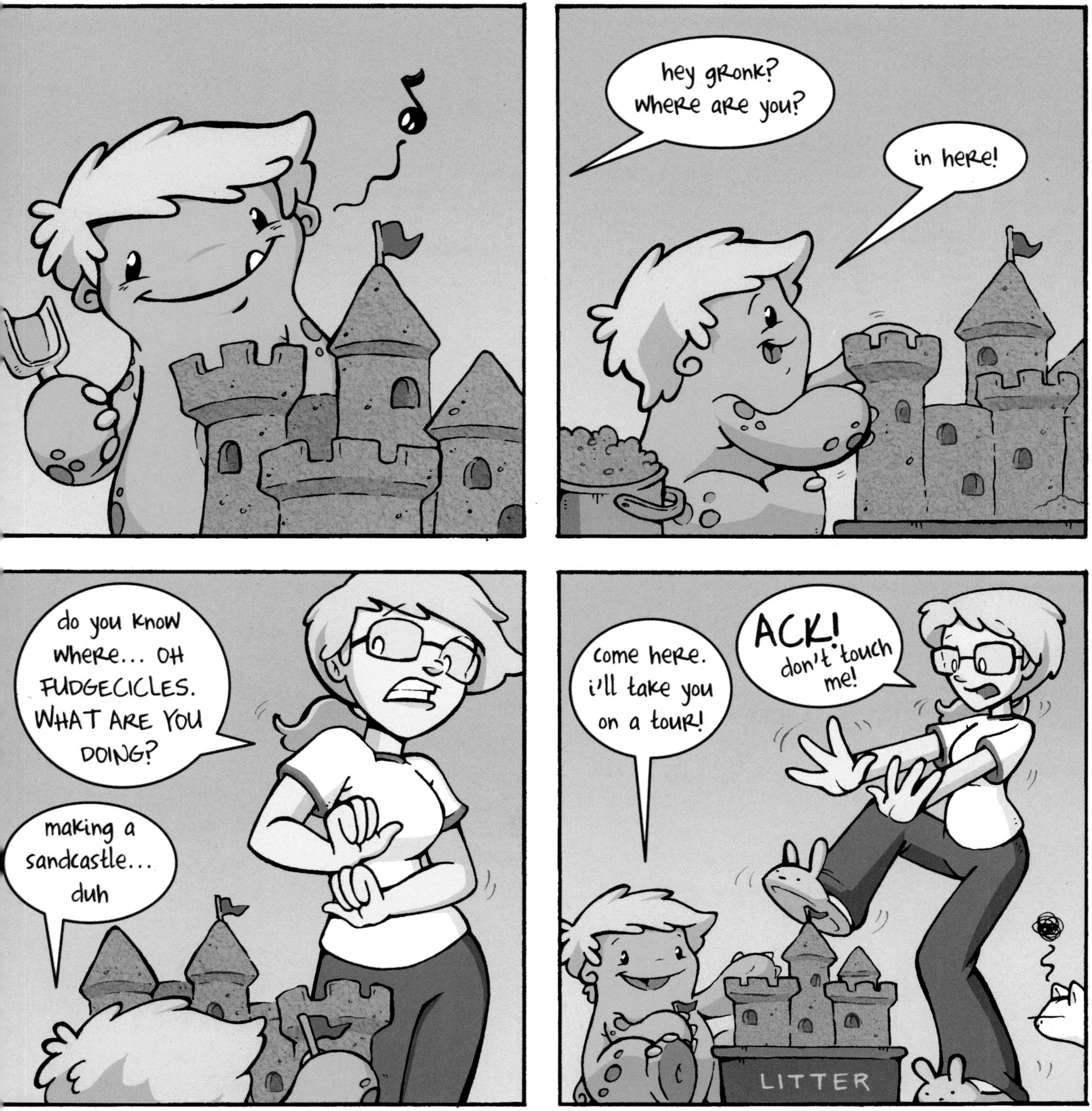
hey gronk? where are you?
in here!
do you know where... OH FUDGECICLES. WHAT ARE YOU DOING?
making a sandcastle... duh
come here. i'll take you on a tour!
ACK! don't touch me!
LITTER

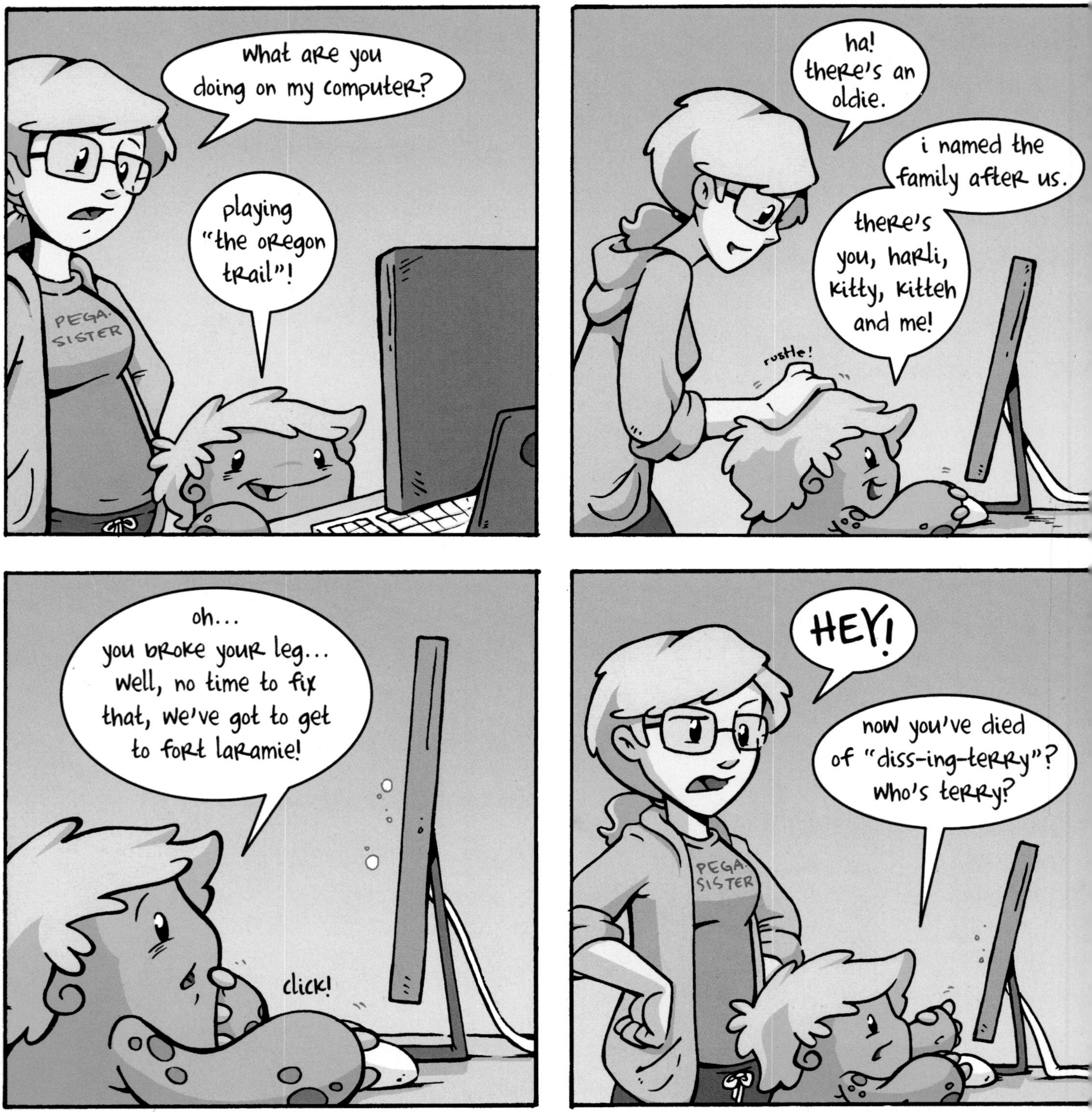
What are you doing on my computer?
playing "the oregon trail"!
PEGA. SISTER
ha! there's an oldie.
i named the family after us.
there's you, harli, kitty, kitteh and me!
rustle!
oh... you broke your leg... well, no time to fix that, we've got to get to fort laramie!
click!
HEY!
now you've died of "diss-ing-terry"? Who's terry?
PEGA. SISTER

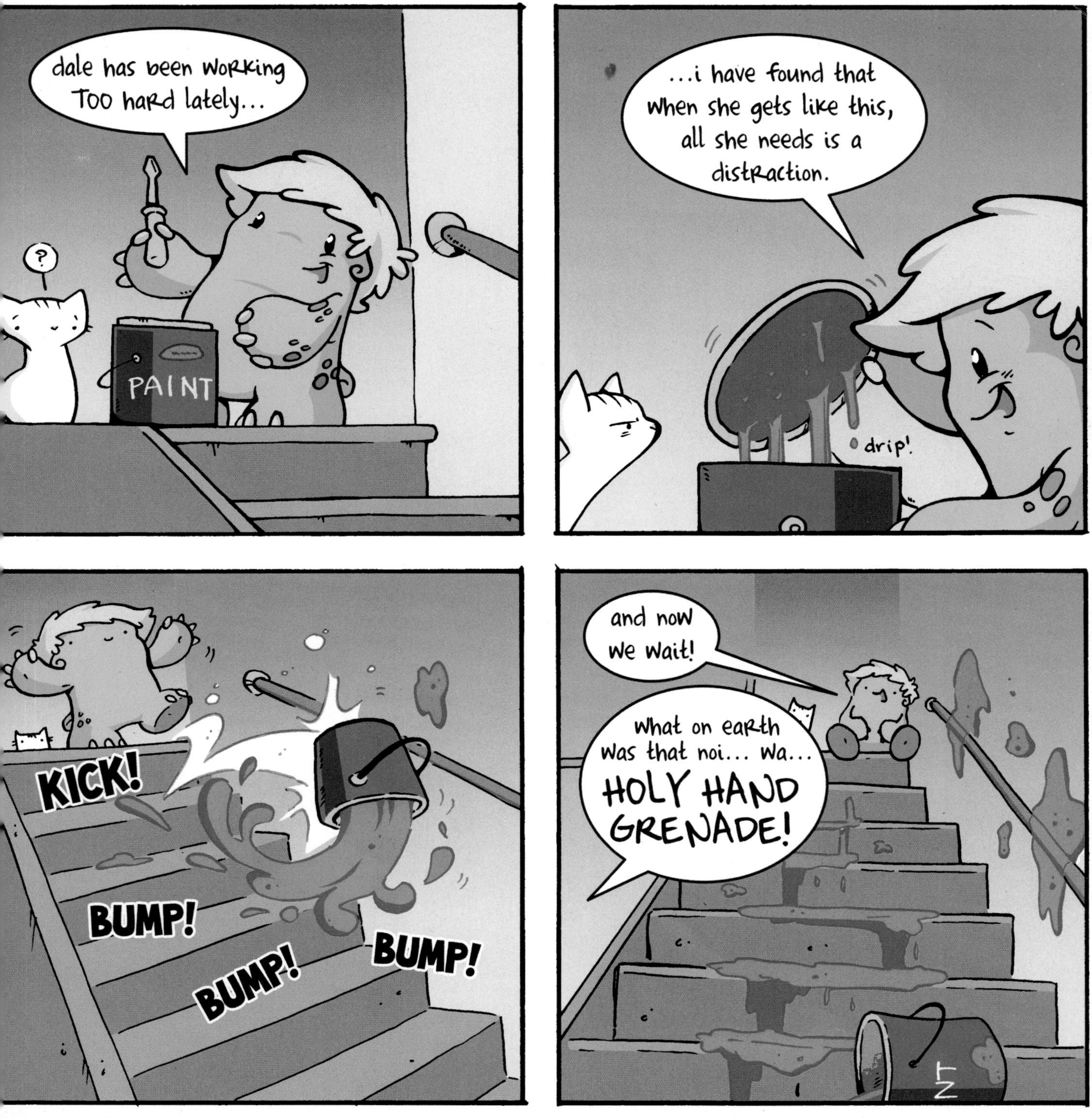
dale has been working TOO hard lately...
?
PAINT
...i have found that when she gets like this, all she needs is a distraction.
drip!
KICK!
BUMP!
BUMP!
BUMP!
and now we wait!
What on earth was that noi... wa... HOLY HAND GRENADE!

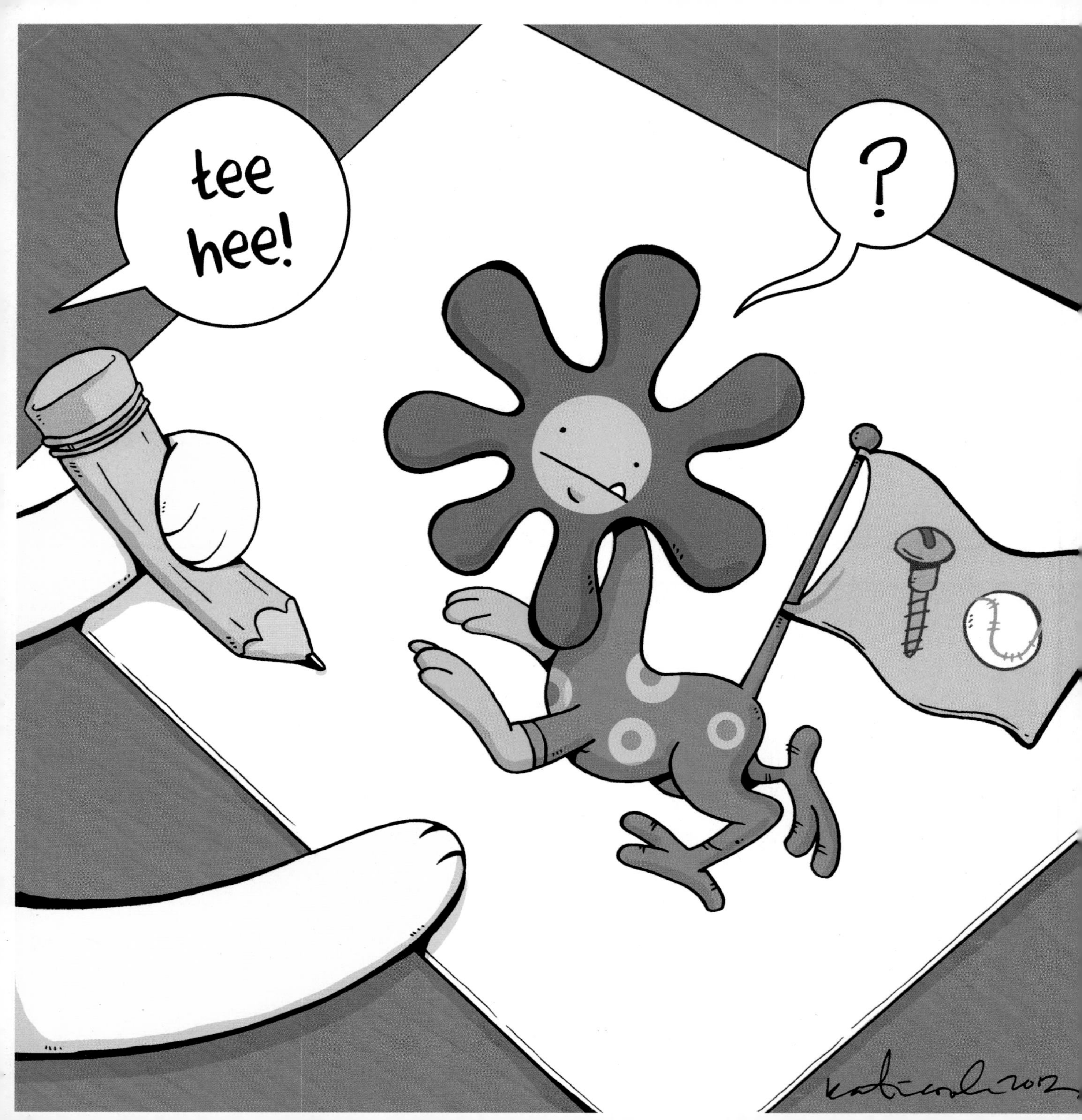
tee hee!
?

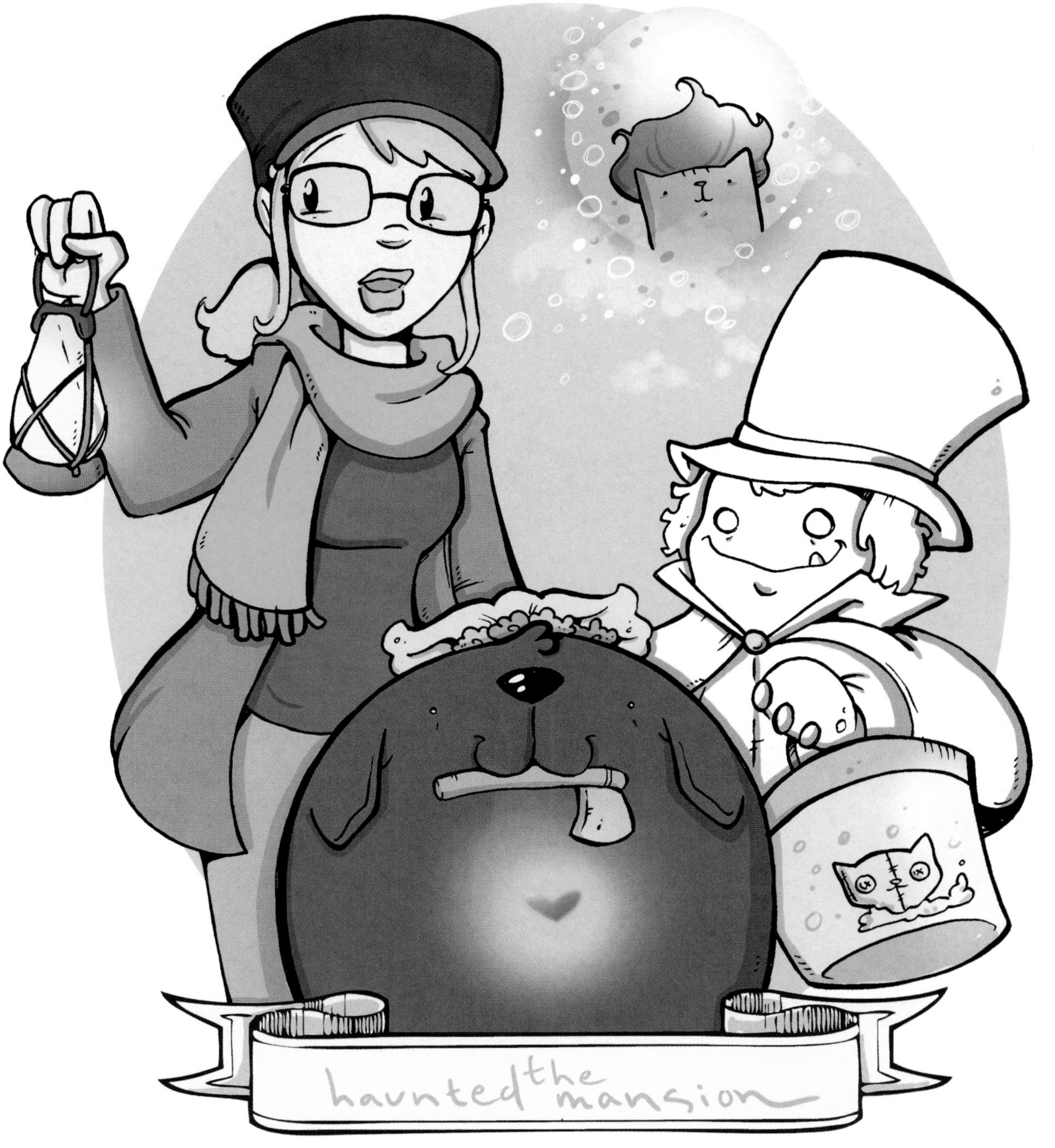
haunted the mansion

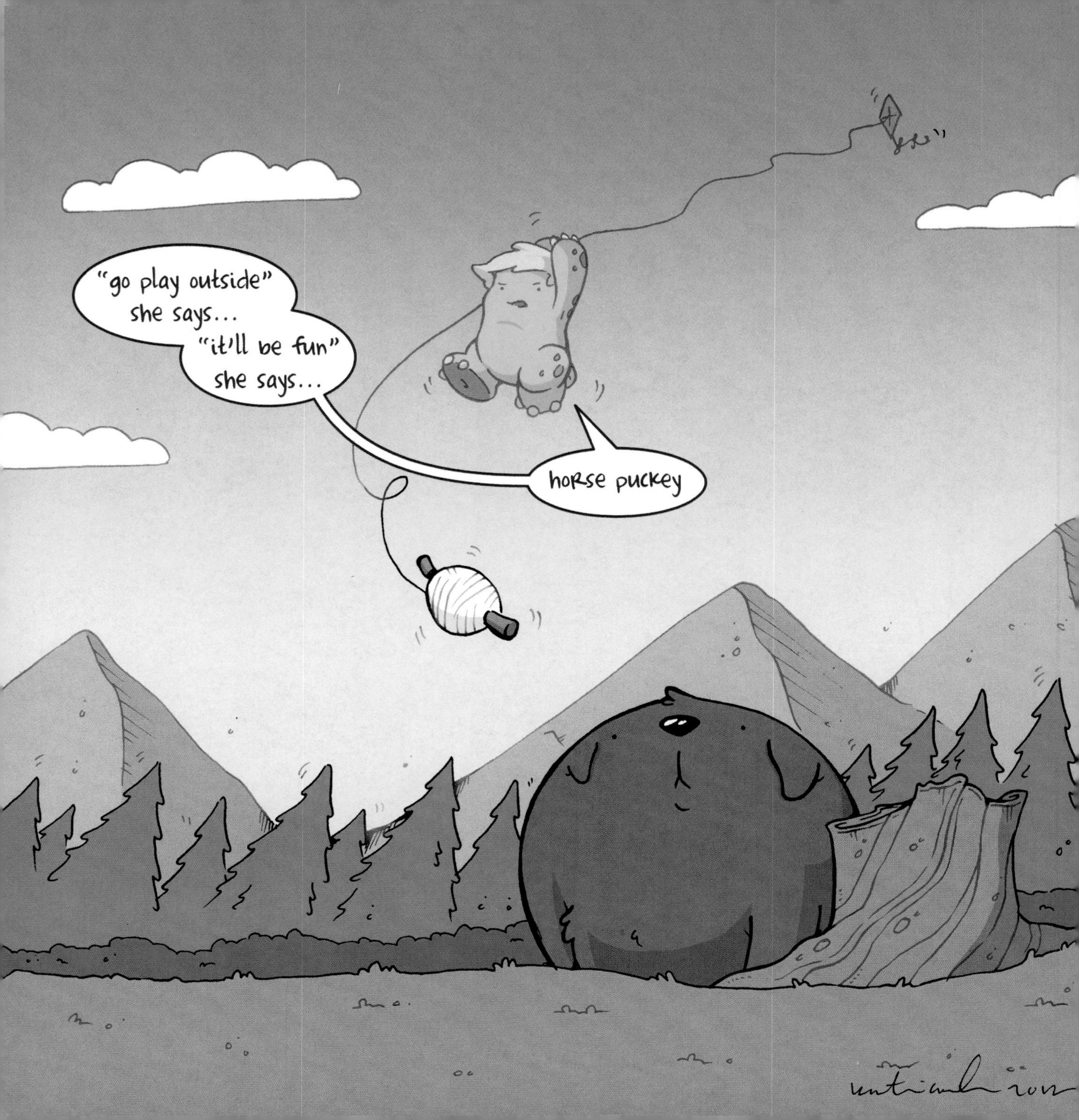
"go play outside" she says...
"it'll be fun" she says...
horse puckey

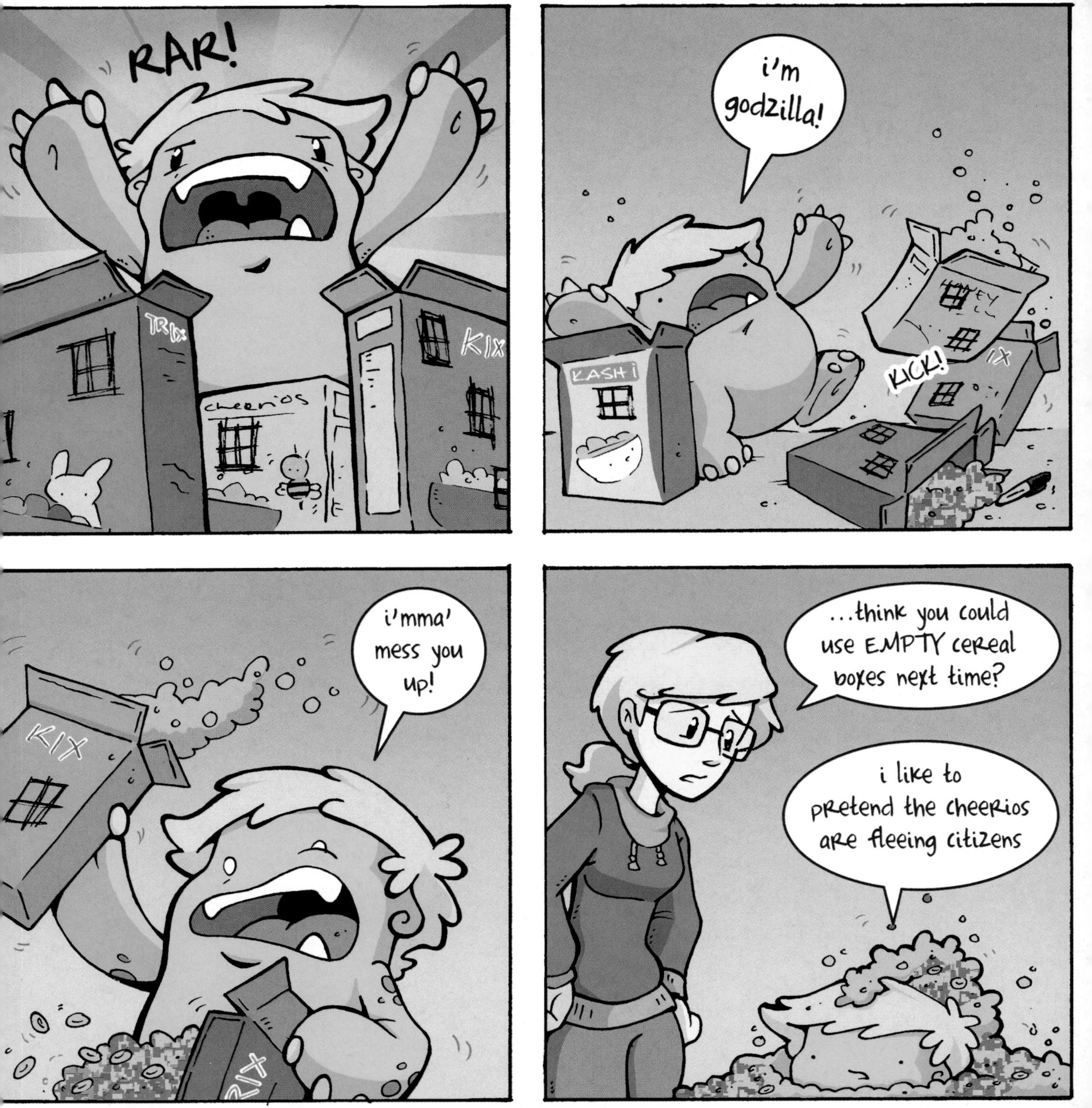
RAR!
TRIX
KIX
cheerios
i'm godzilla!
KASHI
KICK!
i'mma' mess you up!
KIX
...think you could use EMPTY cereal boxes next time?
i like to pretend the cheerios are fleeing citizens

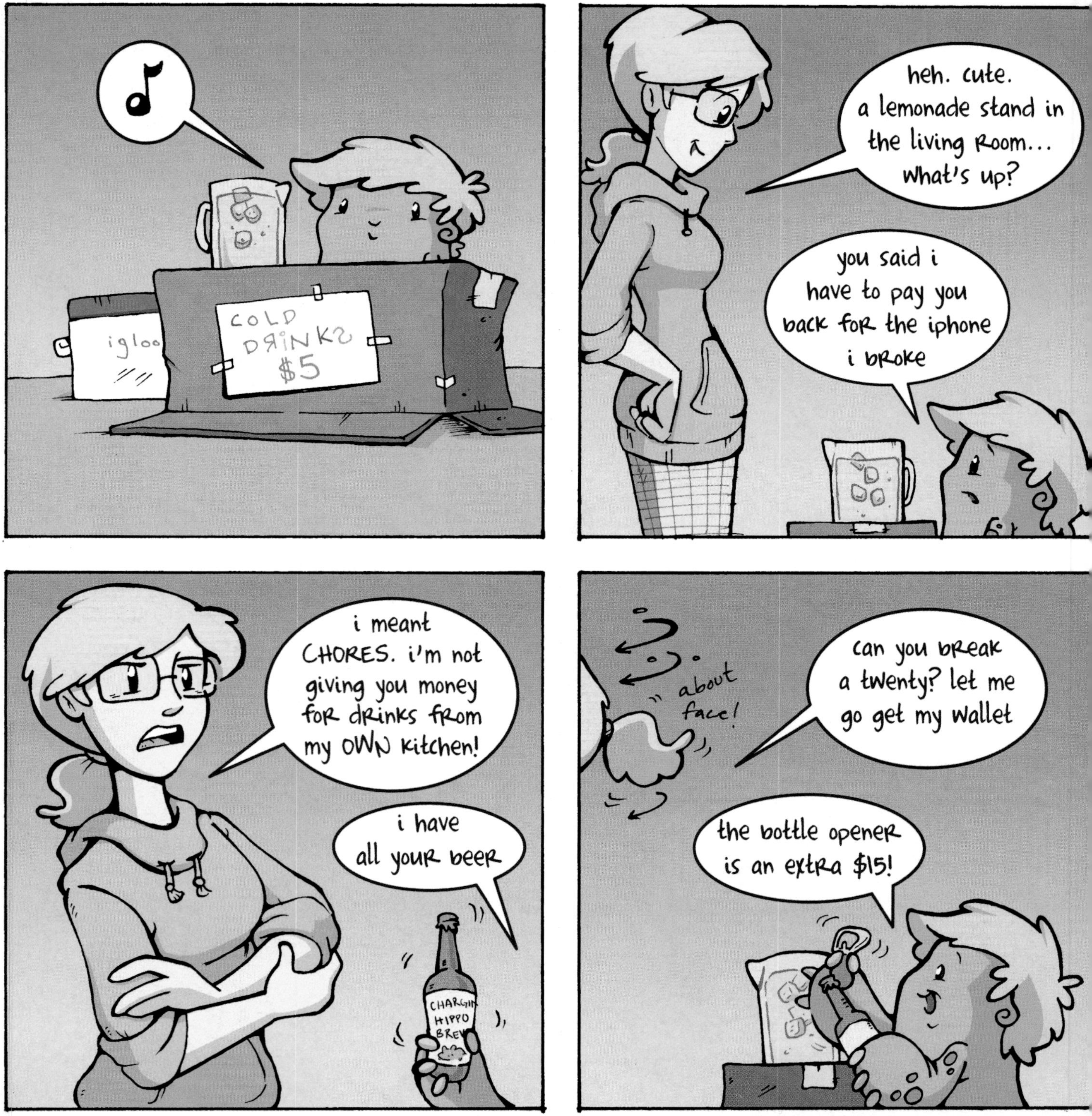
♪
igloo
COLD DRINKS $5
heh. cute. a lemonade stand in the living room... what's up?
you said i have to pay you back for the iphone i broke
i meant CHORES. i'm not giving you money for drinks from my OWN kitchen!
i have all your beer
CHARGIN HIPPO BREW
about face!
can you break a twenty? let me go get my wallet
the bottle opener is an extra $15!

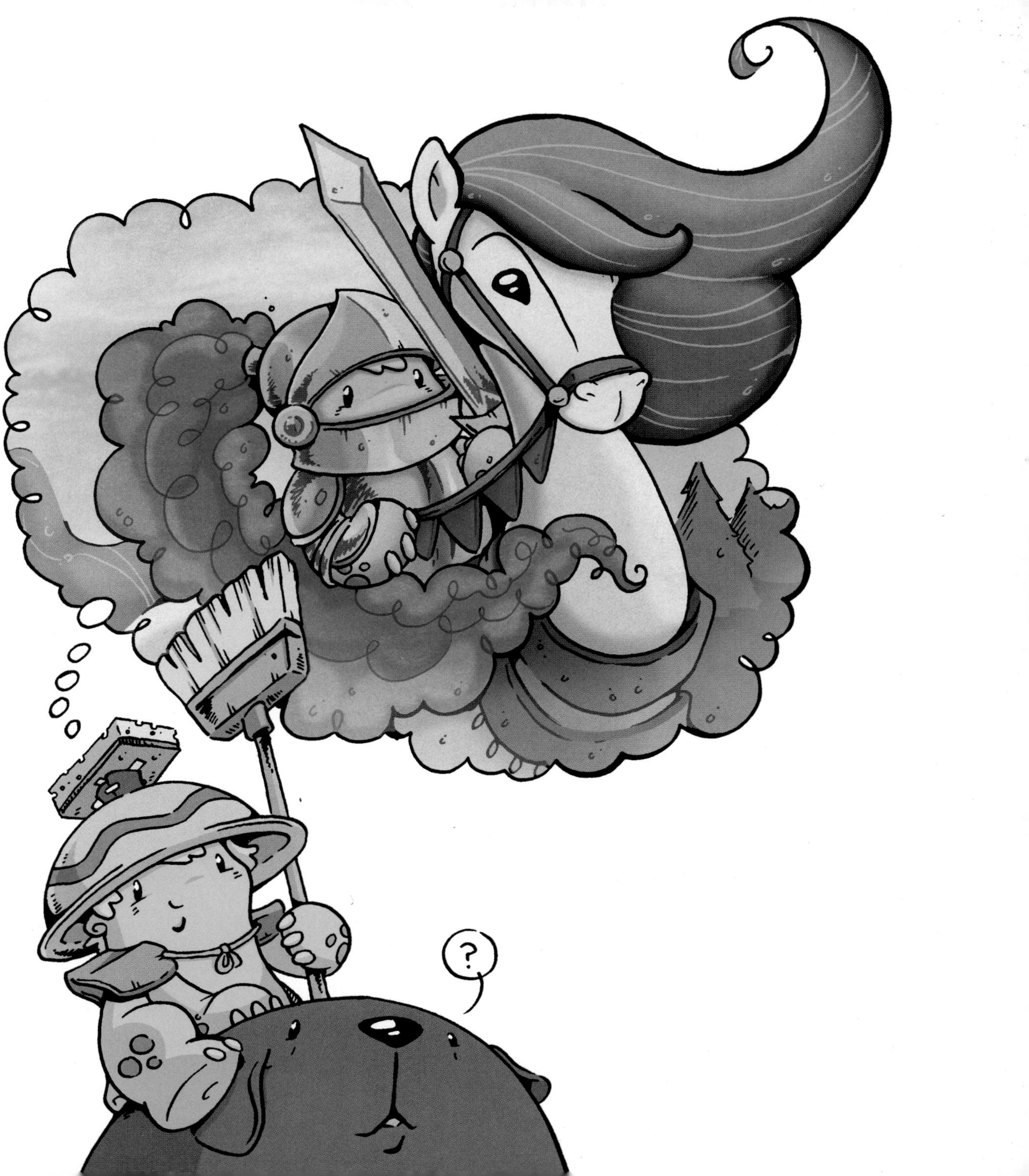
?

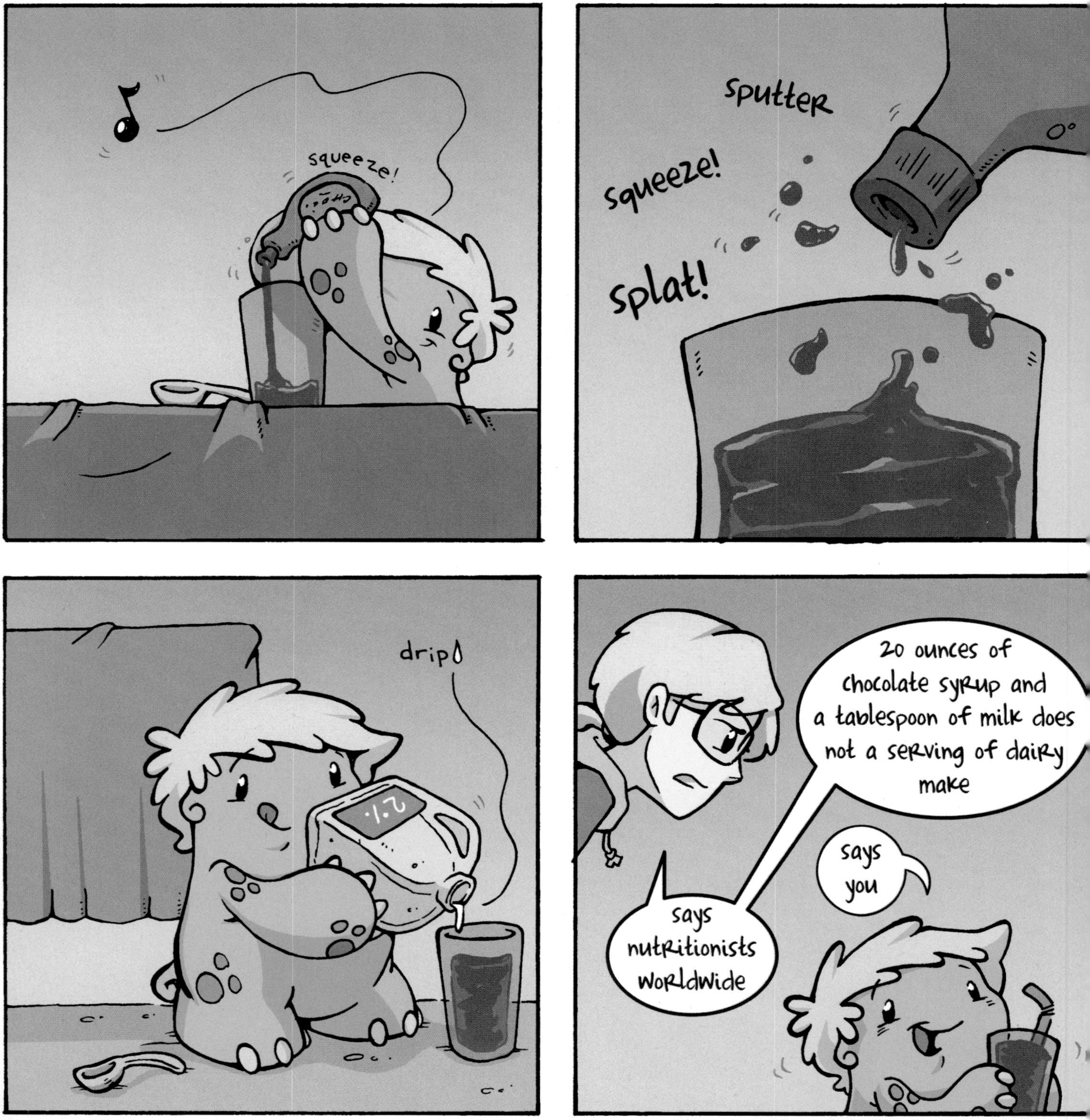
squeeze!
sputter
squeeze!
splat!
drip
20 ounces of chocolate syrup and a tablespoon of milk does not a serving of dairy make
says you
says nutritionists worldwide

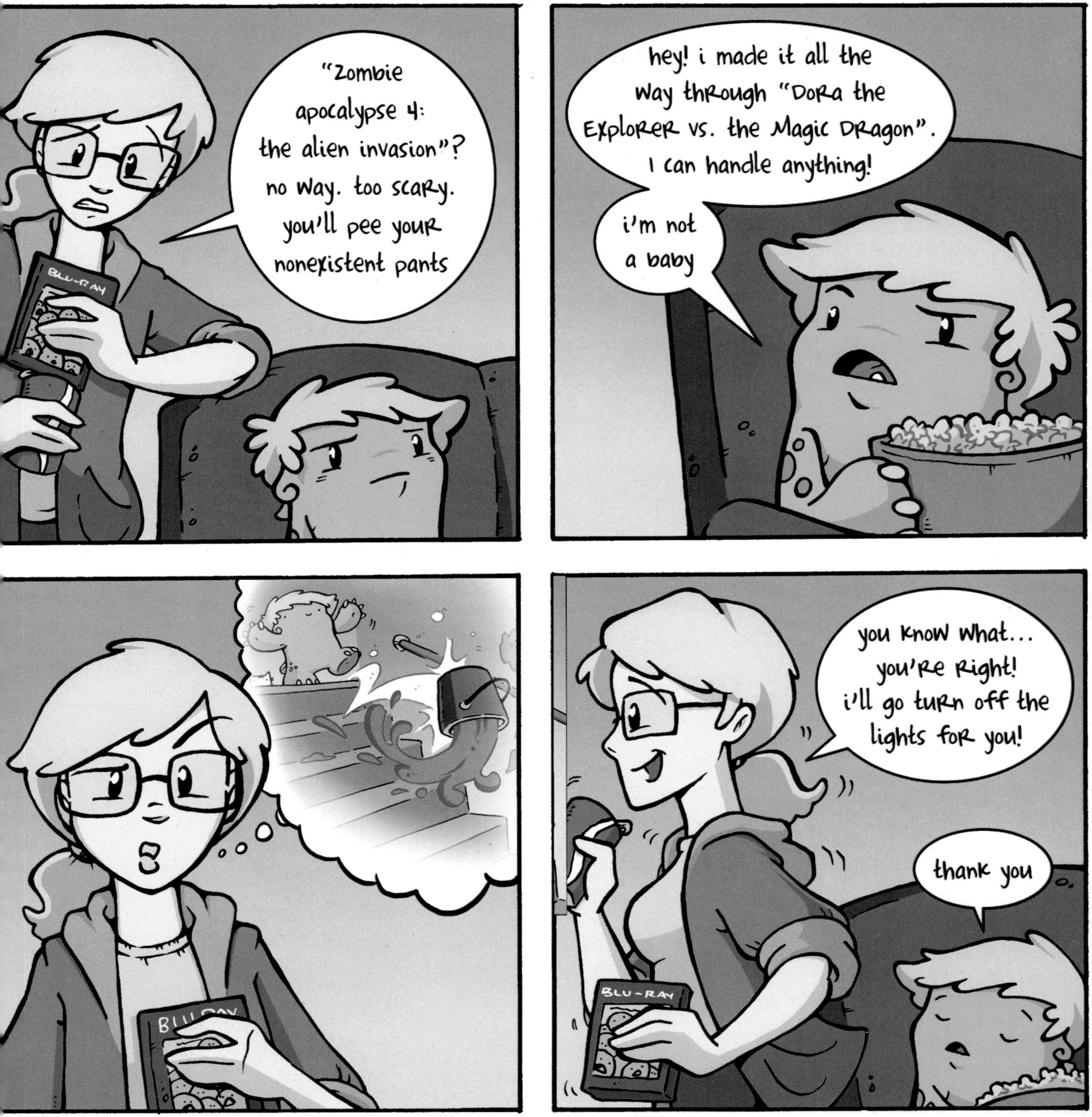
"Zombie apocalypse 4: the alien invasion"? no way. too scary. you'll pee your nonexistent pants
hey! i made it all the way through "Dora the Explorer vs. the Magic Dragon". I can handle anything!
i'm not a baby
BLU-RAY
you know what... you're right! i'll go turn off the lights for you!
thank you
BLU-RAY

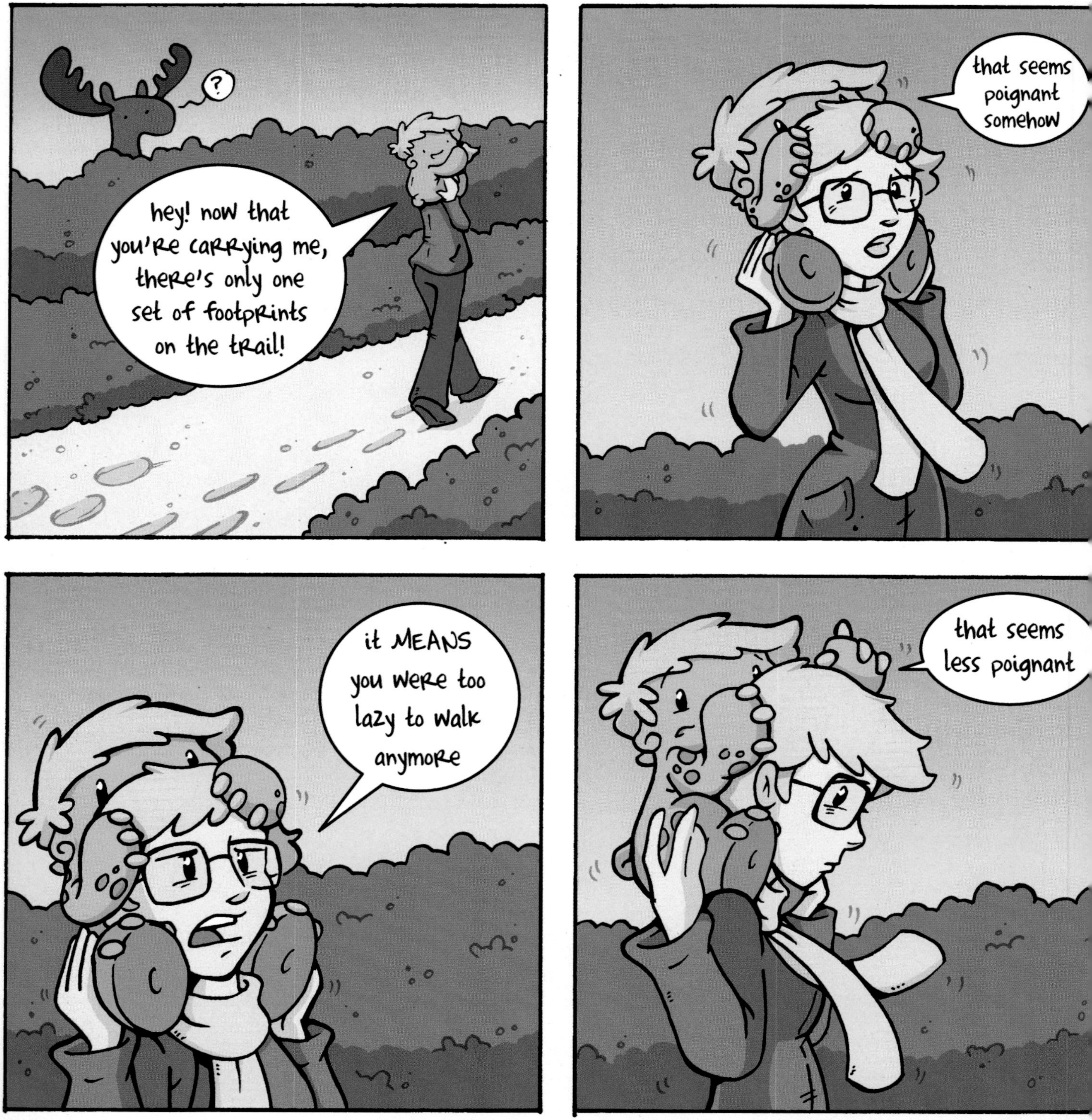
?
hey! now that you're carrying me, there's only one set of footprints on the trail!
that seems poignant somehow
it MEANS you were too lazy to walk anymore
that seems less poignant

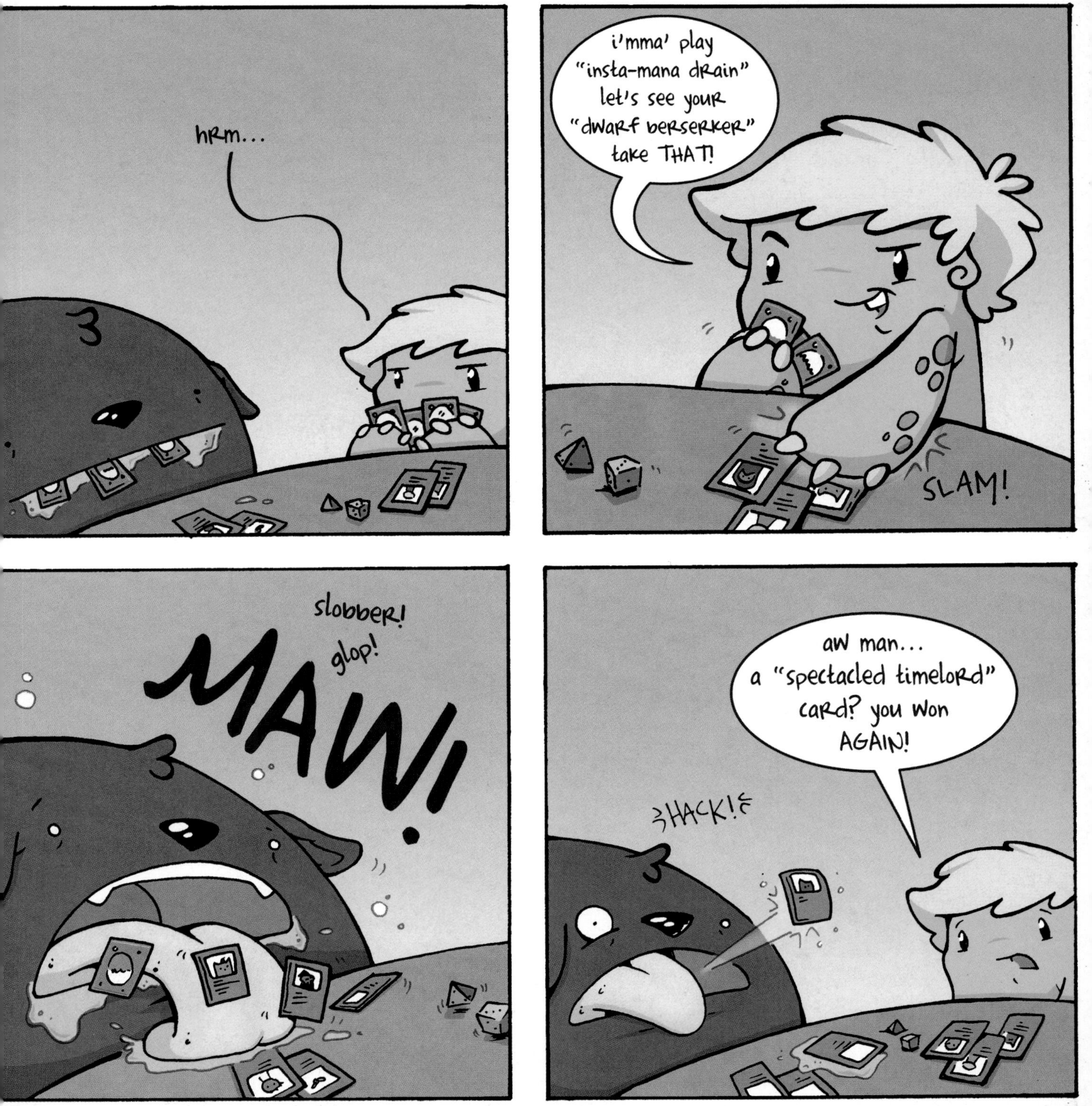

hrm...
i'mma' play "insta-mana drain" let's see your "dwarf berserker" take THAT!
SLAM!
slobber!
glop!
MAW!
HACK!
aw man... a "spectacled timelord" card? you won AGAIN!

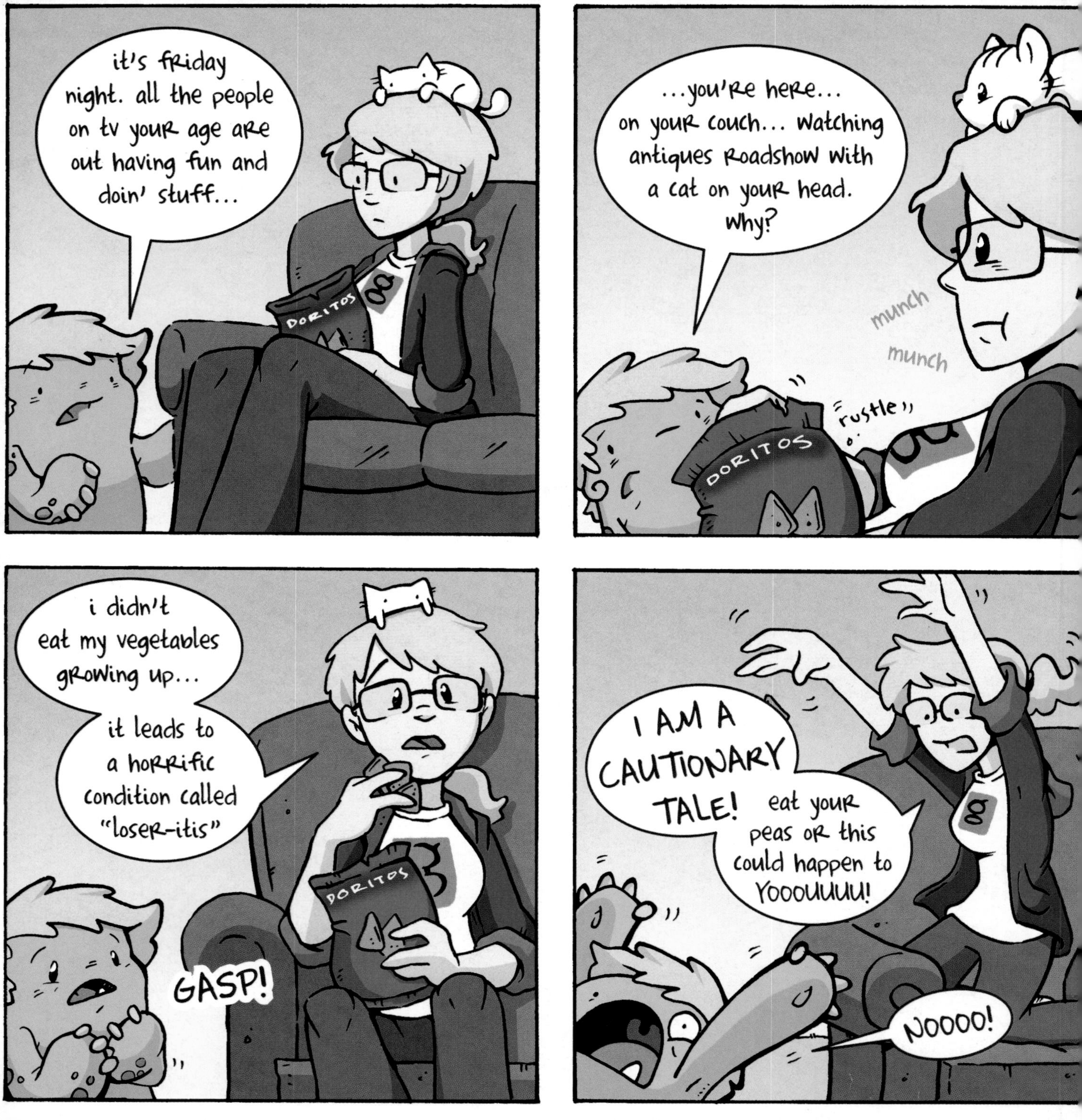
it's friday night. all the people on tv your age are out having fun and doin' stuff...
...you're here... on your couch... watching antiques roadshow with a cat on your head. why?
munch
munch
rustle
DORITOS
i didn't eat my vegetables growing up...
it leads to a horrific condition called "loser-itis"
GASP!
DORITOS
I AM A CAUTIONARY TALE!
eat your peas or this could happen to YOOOUUUU!
NOOOO!

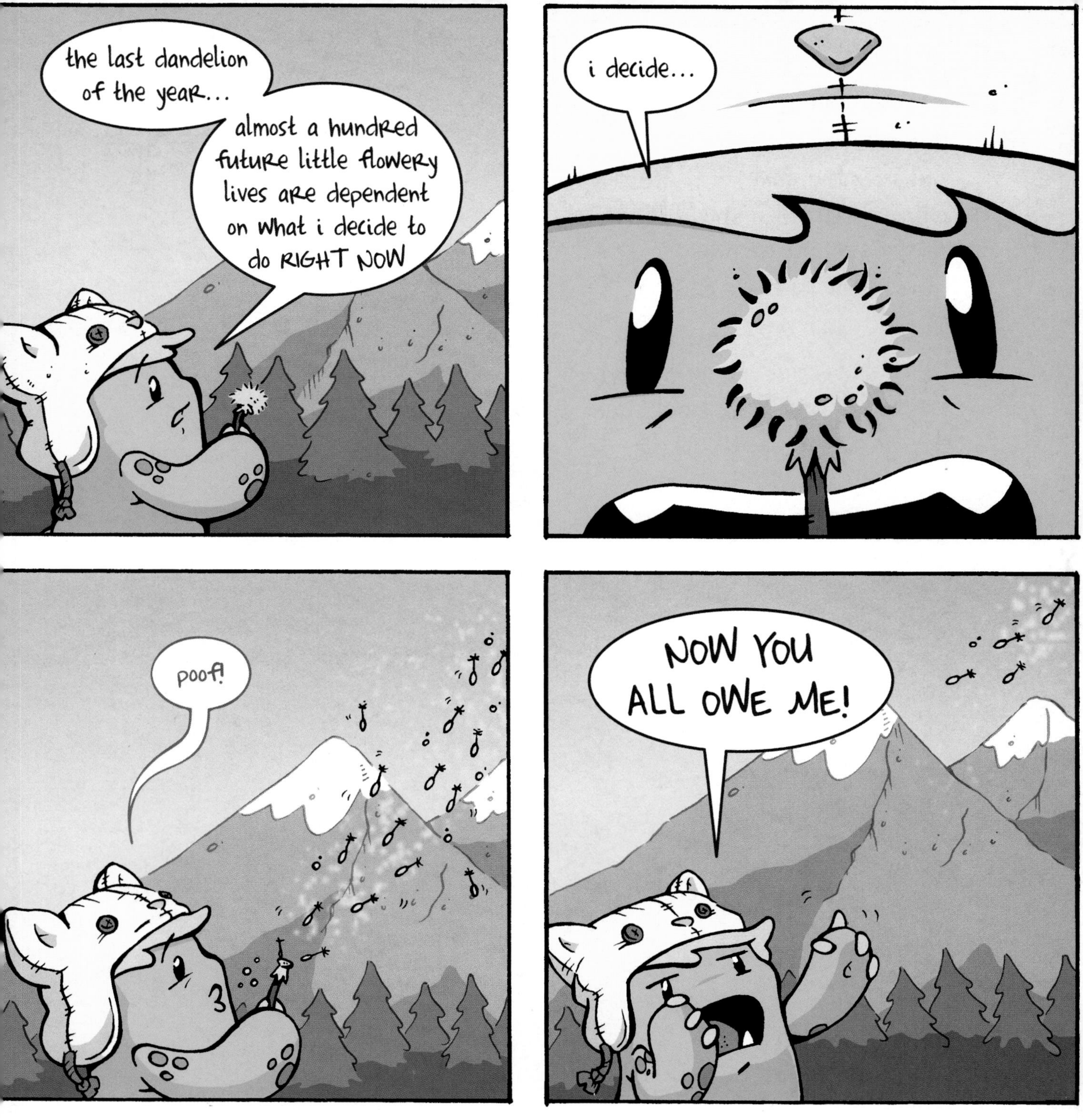
the last dandelion of the year...
almost a hundred future little flowery lives are dependent on what i decide to do RIGHT NOW
i decide...
poof!
NOW YOU ALL OWE ME!

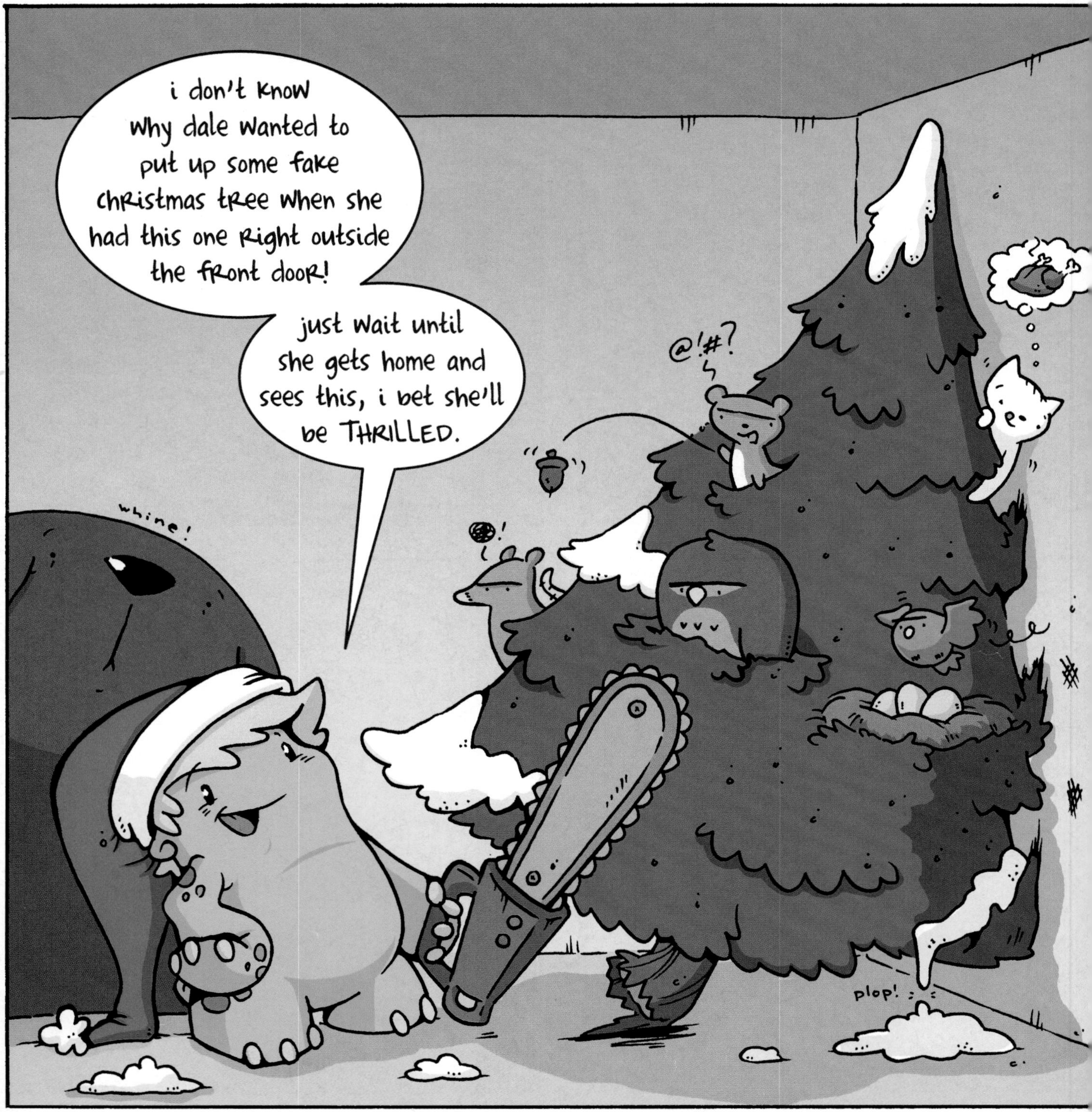
i don't know why dale wanted to put up some fake christmas tree when she had this one right outside the front door!
just wait until she gets home and sees this, i bet she'll be THRILLED.
@!#?
whine!
plop!

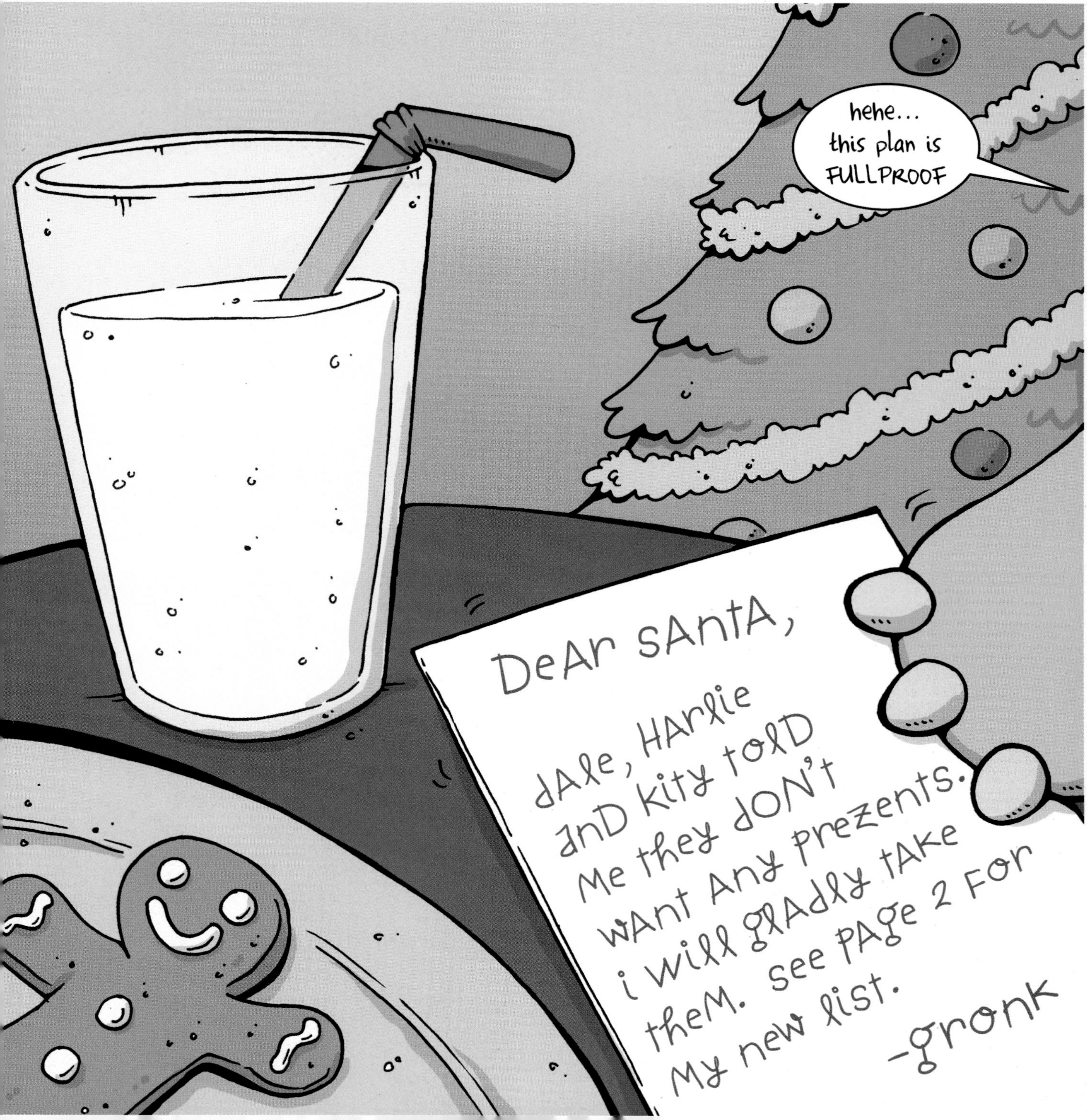
hehe...
this plan is
FULLPROOF
DeAr SAntA,
dAle, HArlie
And Kity tolD
Me they dON't
wAnt Any prezents.
i Will glAdly tAke
theM. see PAge 2 For
My new list.
-gronk

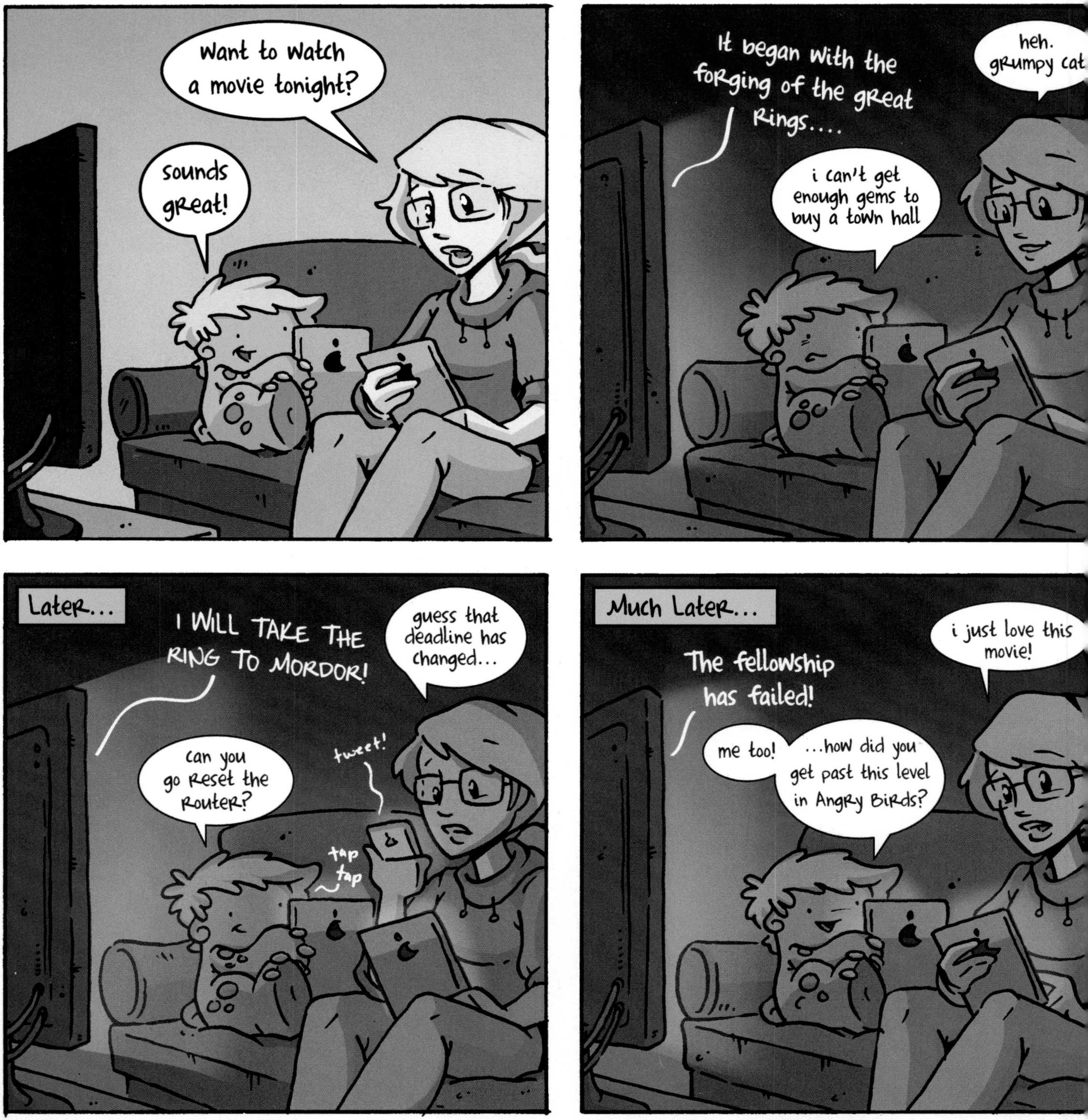
Want to watch a movie tonight?
sounds great!
It began with the forging of the great Rings....
heh. grumpy cat
i can't get enough gems to buy a town hall
Later...
I WILL TAKE THE RING TO MORDOR!
guess that deadline has changed...
can you go reset the router?
tweet!
tap tap
Much Later...
The fellowship has failed!
i just love this movie!
me too!
...how did you get past this level in Angry Birds?

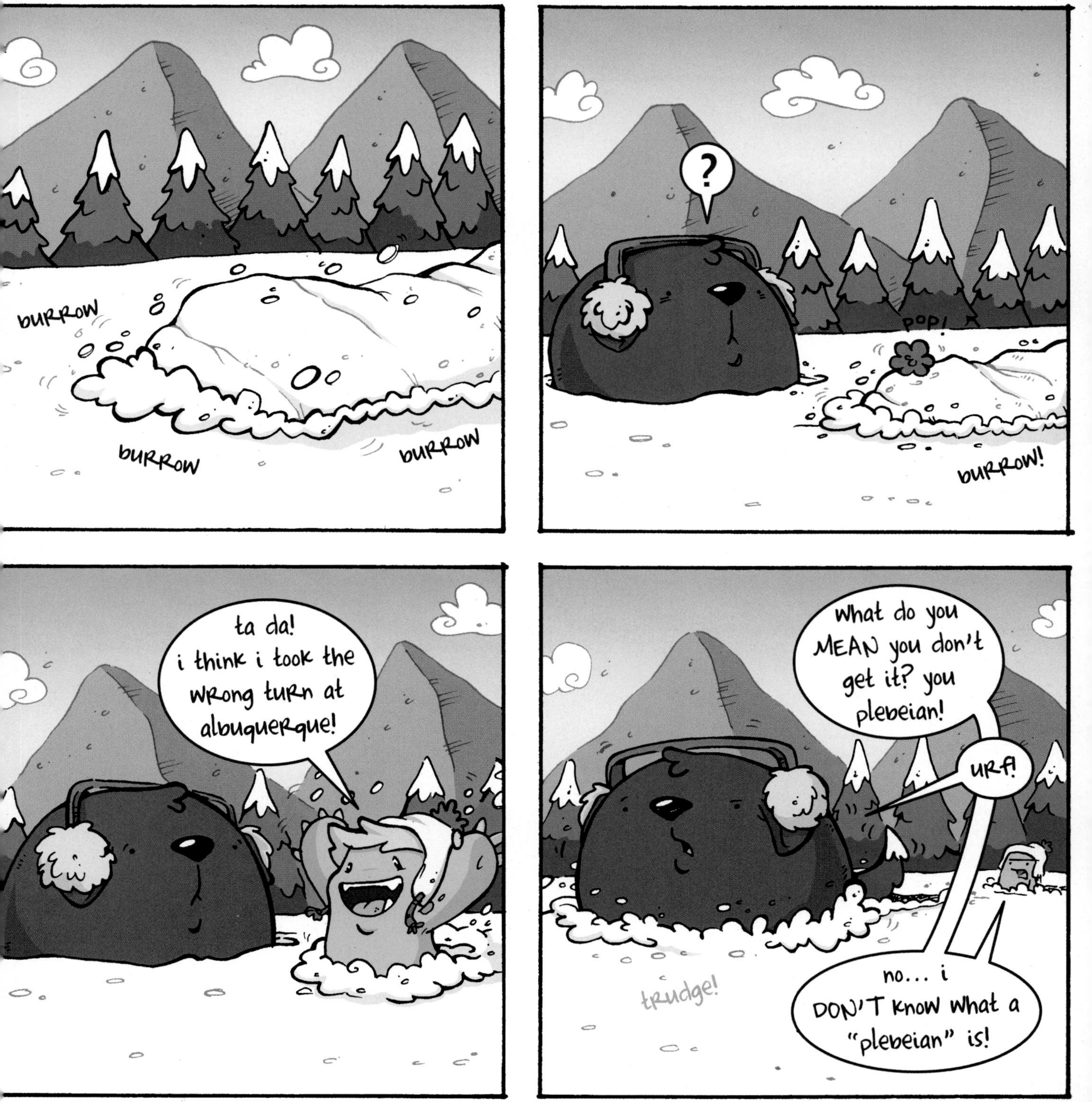
burrow
burrow
burrow
?
pop!
burrow!
ta da!
i think i took the wrong turn at albuquerque!
What do you MEAN you don't get it? you plebeian!
URF!
trudge!
no... i DON'T know what a "plebeian" is!

hang in there... 'cause, you know...
falling on your bum on top of
your dog is no fun

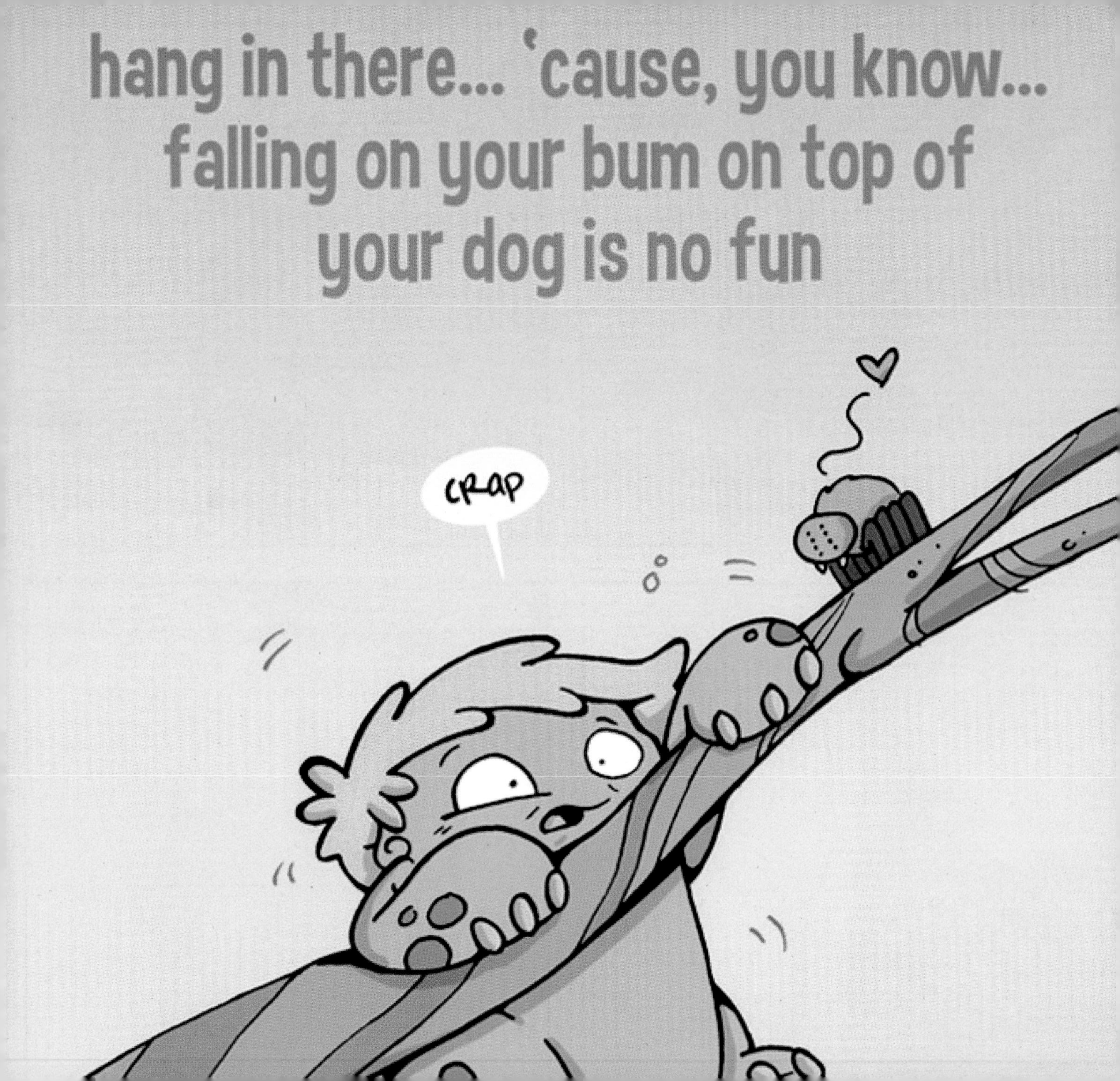
CRAP

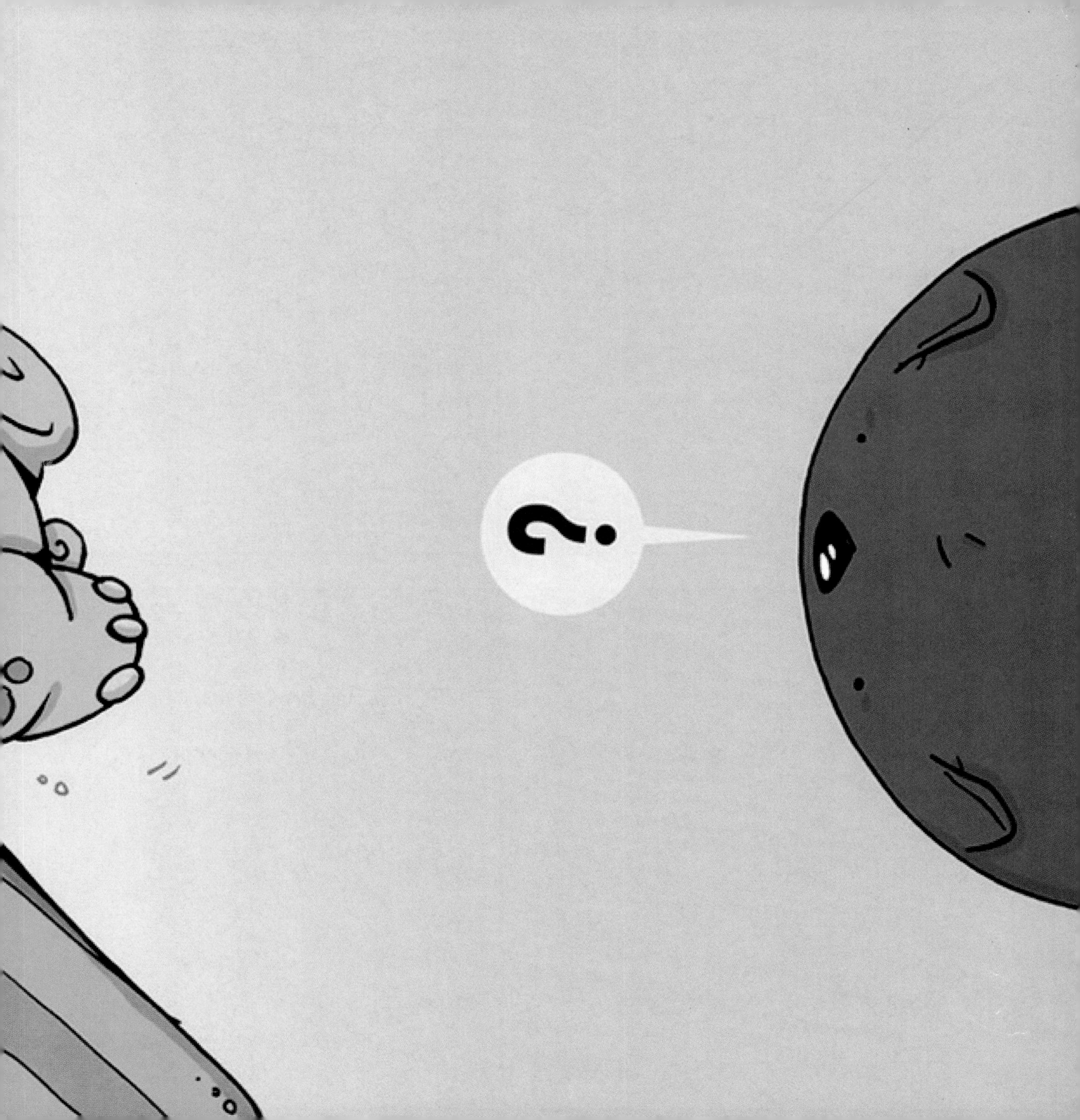
?

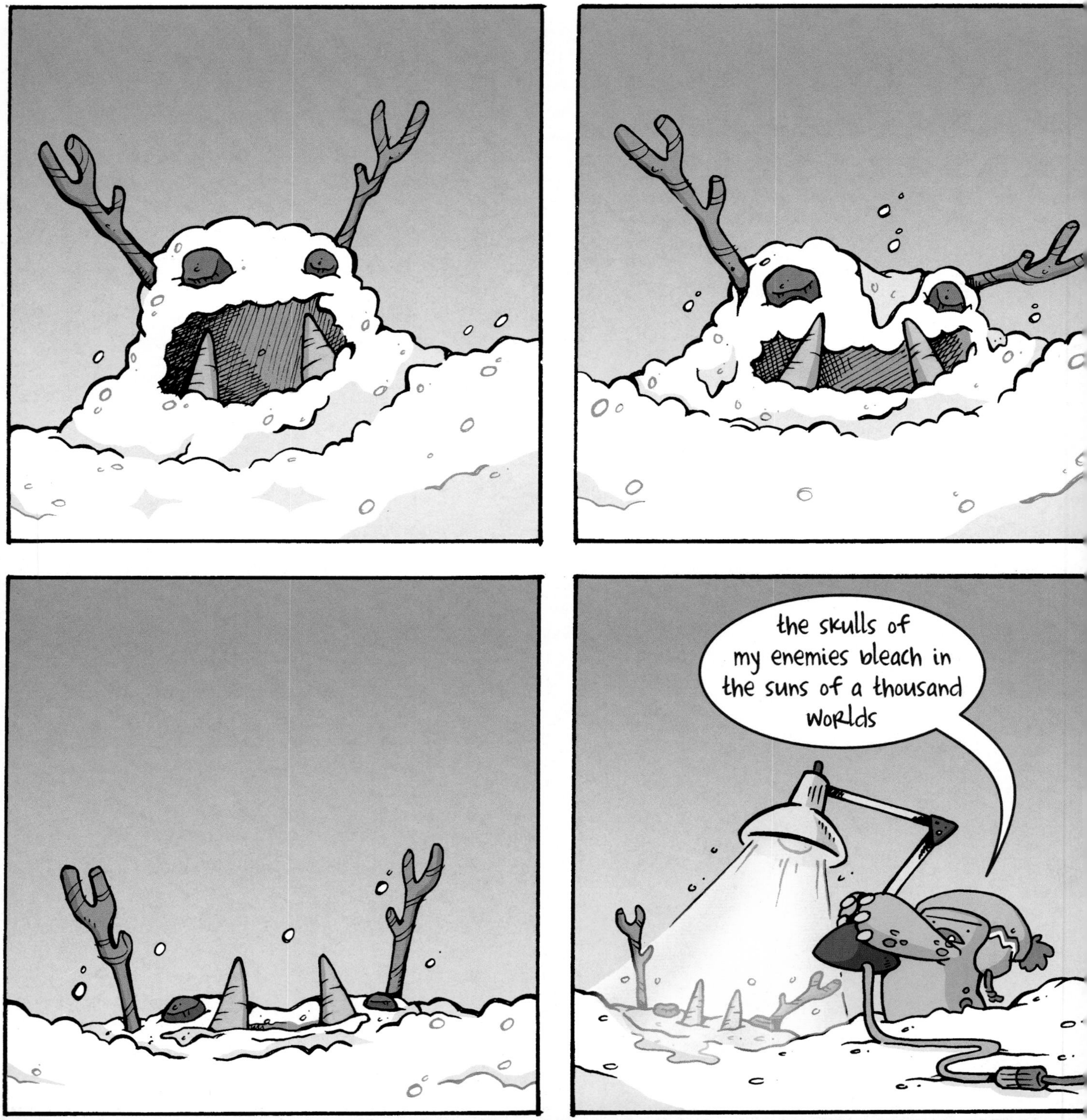
the skulls of my enemies bleach in the suns of a thousand worlds

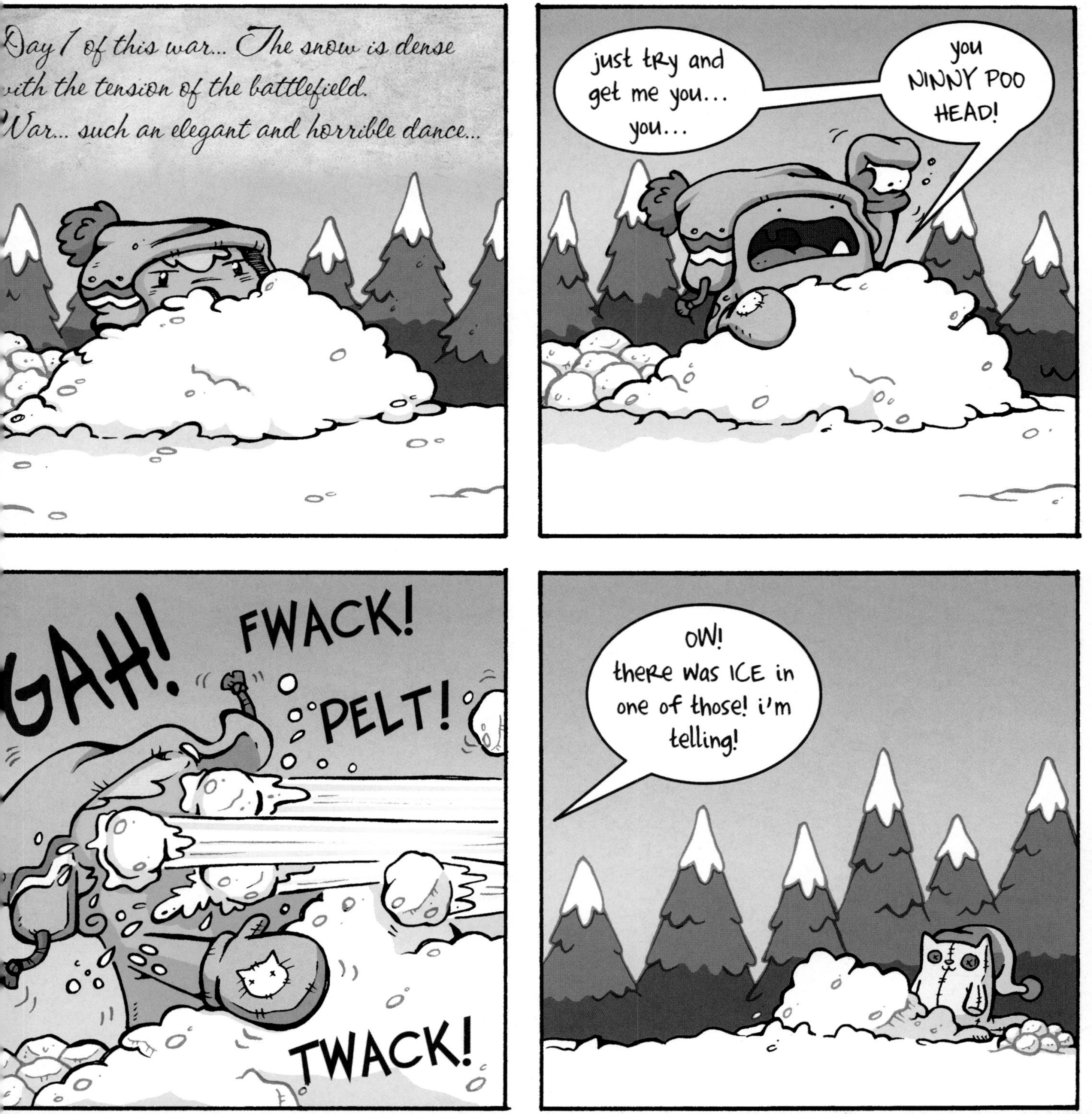
Day 1 of this war... The snow is dense with the tension of the battlefield. War... such an elegant and horrible dance...
just tRy and get me you... you...
you NINNY POO HEAD!
GAH!
FWACK!
PELT!
TWACK!
OW! there was ICE in one of those! i'm telling!

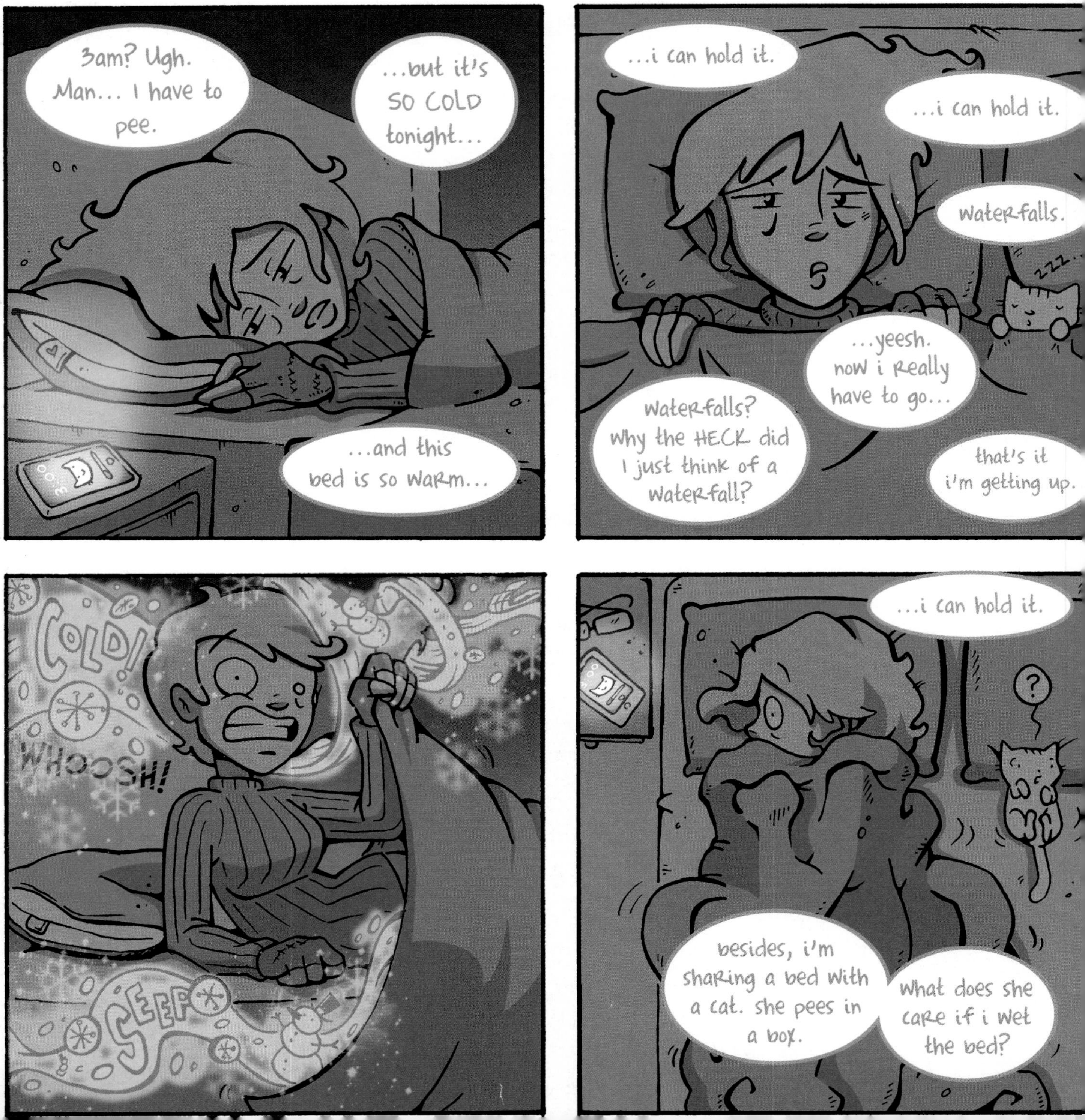
3am? Ugh. Man... I have to pee.
...but it's SO COLD tonight...
...and this bed is so warm...
...i can hold it.
...i can hold it.
Waterfalls.
zzz...
Waterfalls? Why the HECK did I just think of a waterfall?
...yeesh. now i really have to go...
that's it i'm getting up.
COLD!
WHOOSH!
SEEP
...i can hold it.
?
besides, i'm sharing a bed with a cat. she pees in a box.
What does she care if i wet the bed?

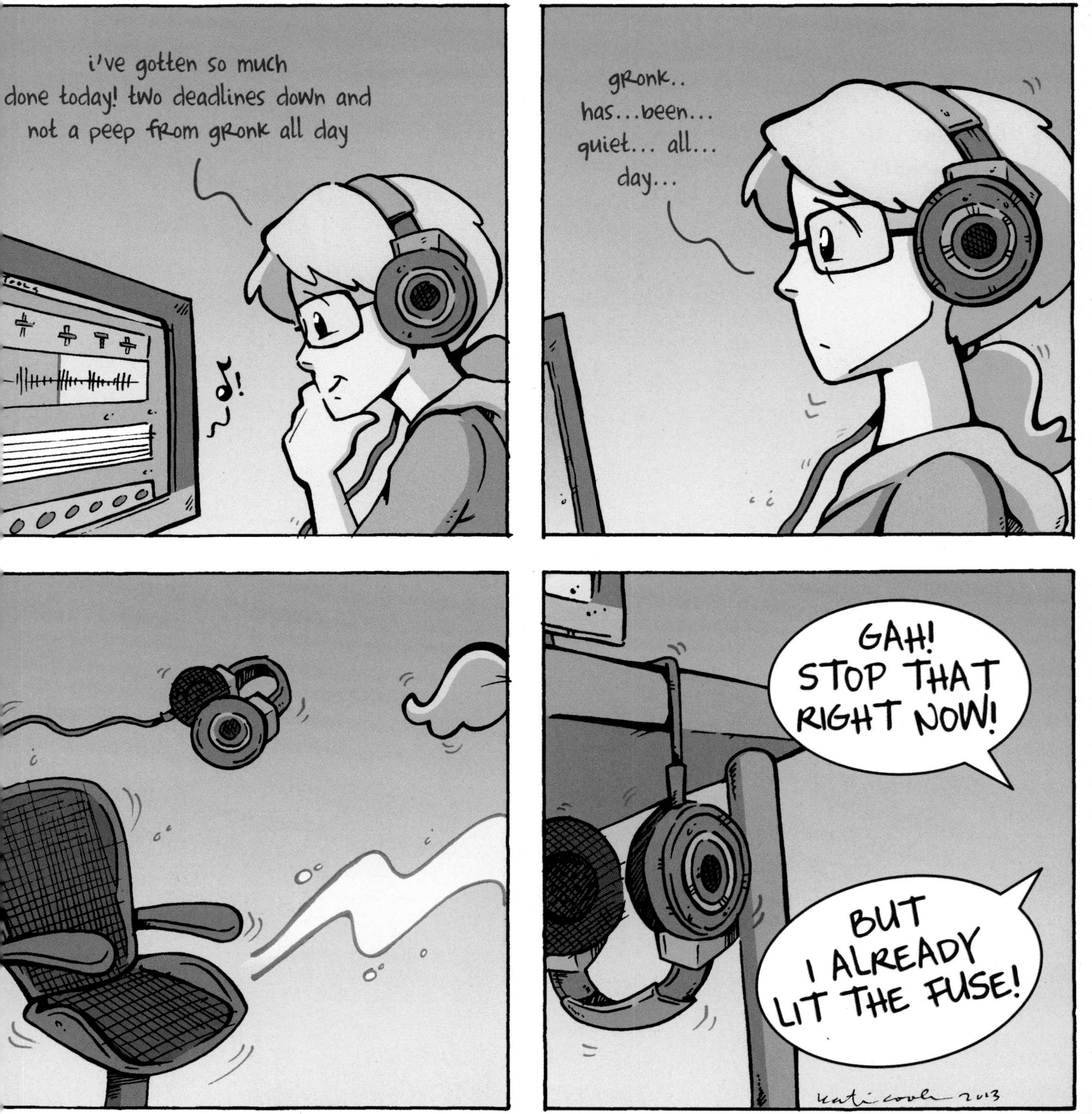
i've gotten so much done today! two deadlines down and not a peep from gronk all day
gronk.. has...been... quiet... all... day...
GAH! STOP THAT RIGHT NOW!
BUT I ALREADY LIT THE FUSE!
katie cook 2013

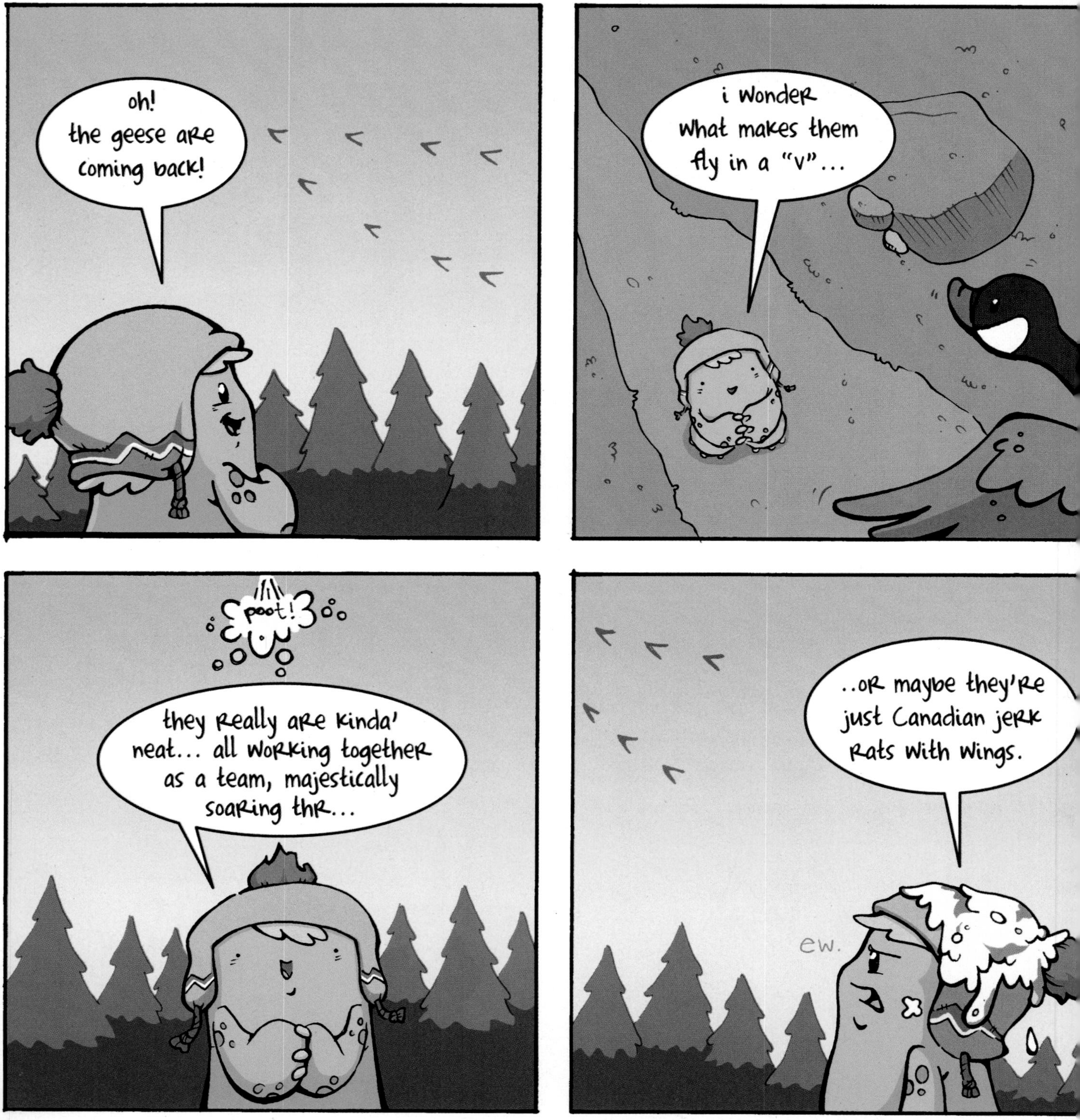
oh!
the geese are
coming back!
i wonder
what makes them
fly in a "v"...
poot!
they really are kinda'
neat... all working together
as a team, majestically
soaring thr...
..or maybe they're
just Canadian jerk
rats with wings.
ew.

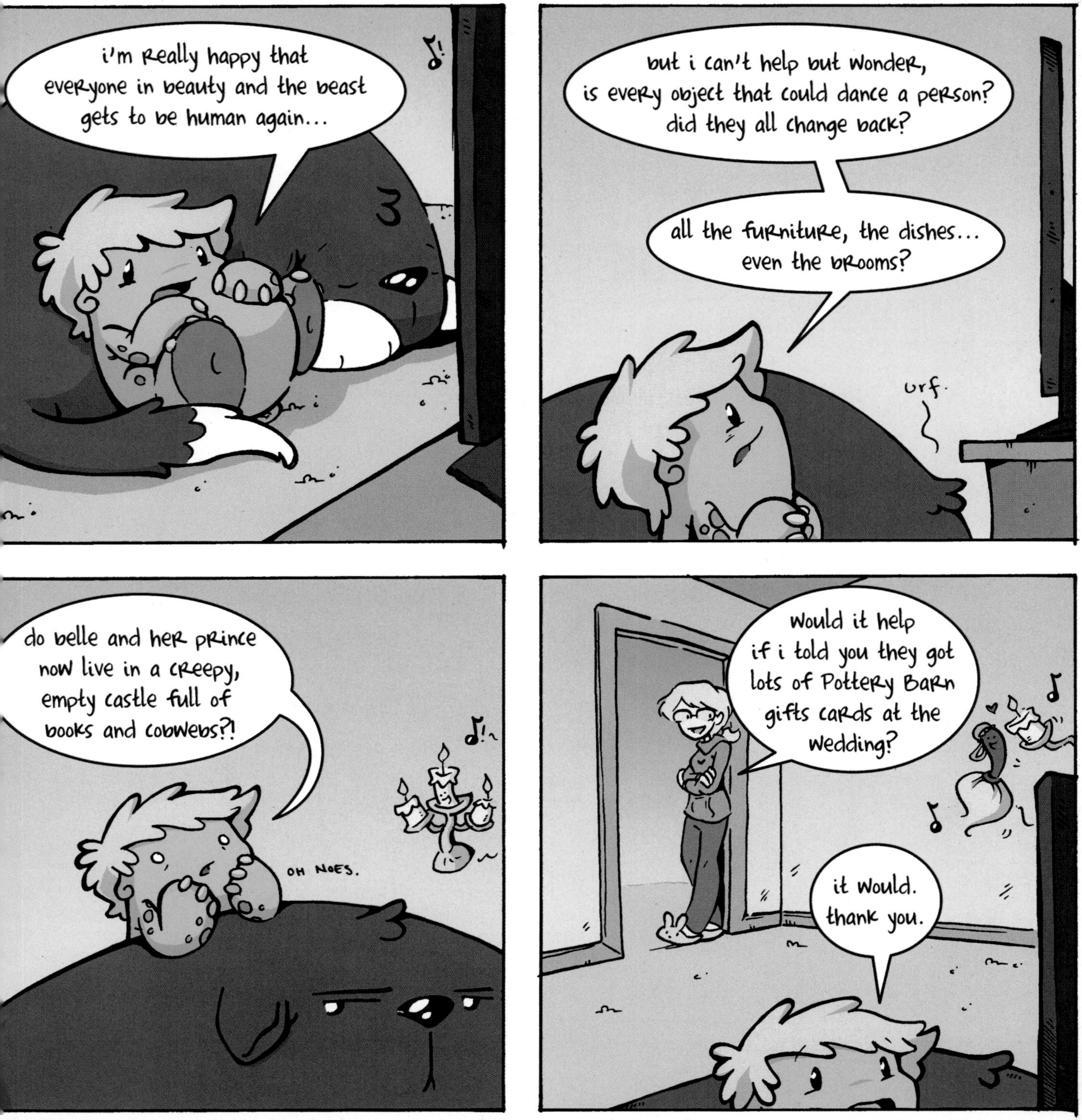
i'm really happy that everyone in beauty and the beast gets to be human again...
but i can't help but wonder, is every object that could dance a person? did they all change back?
all the furniture, the dishes... even the brooms?
urf.
do belle and her prince now live in a creepy, empty castle full of books and cobwebs?!
OH NOES.
Would it help if i told you they got lots of Pottery Barn gifts cards at the wedding?
it would. thank you.

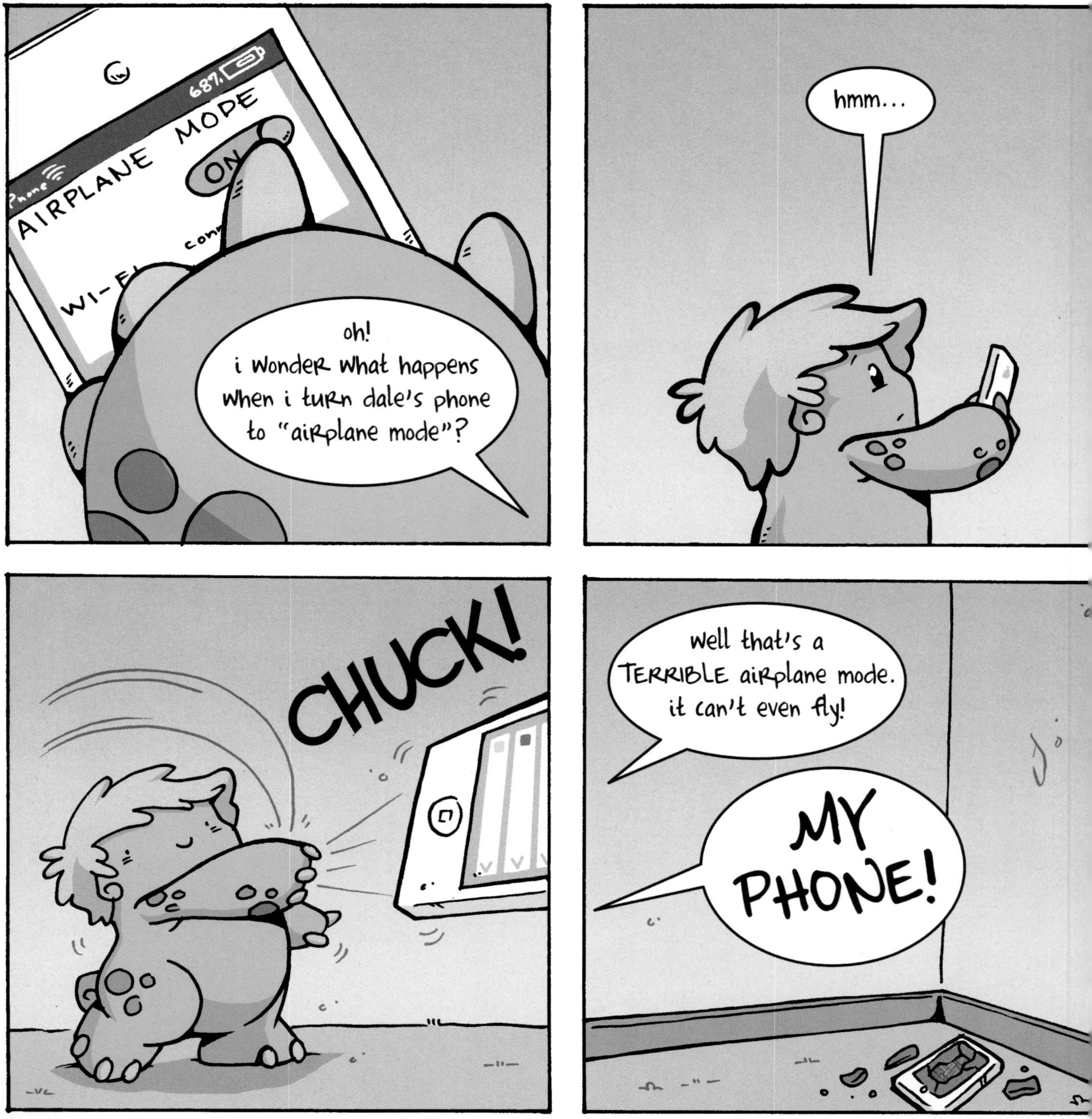
AIRPLANE MODE
ON
WI-FI
oh!
i wonder what happens when i turn dale's phone to "airplane mode"?
hmm...
CHUCK!
well that's a TERRIBLE airplane mode. it can't even fly!
MY PHONE!

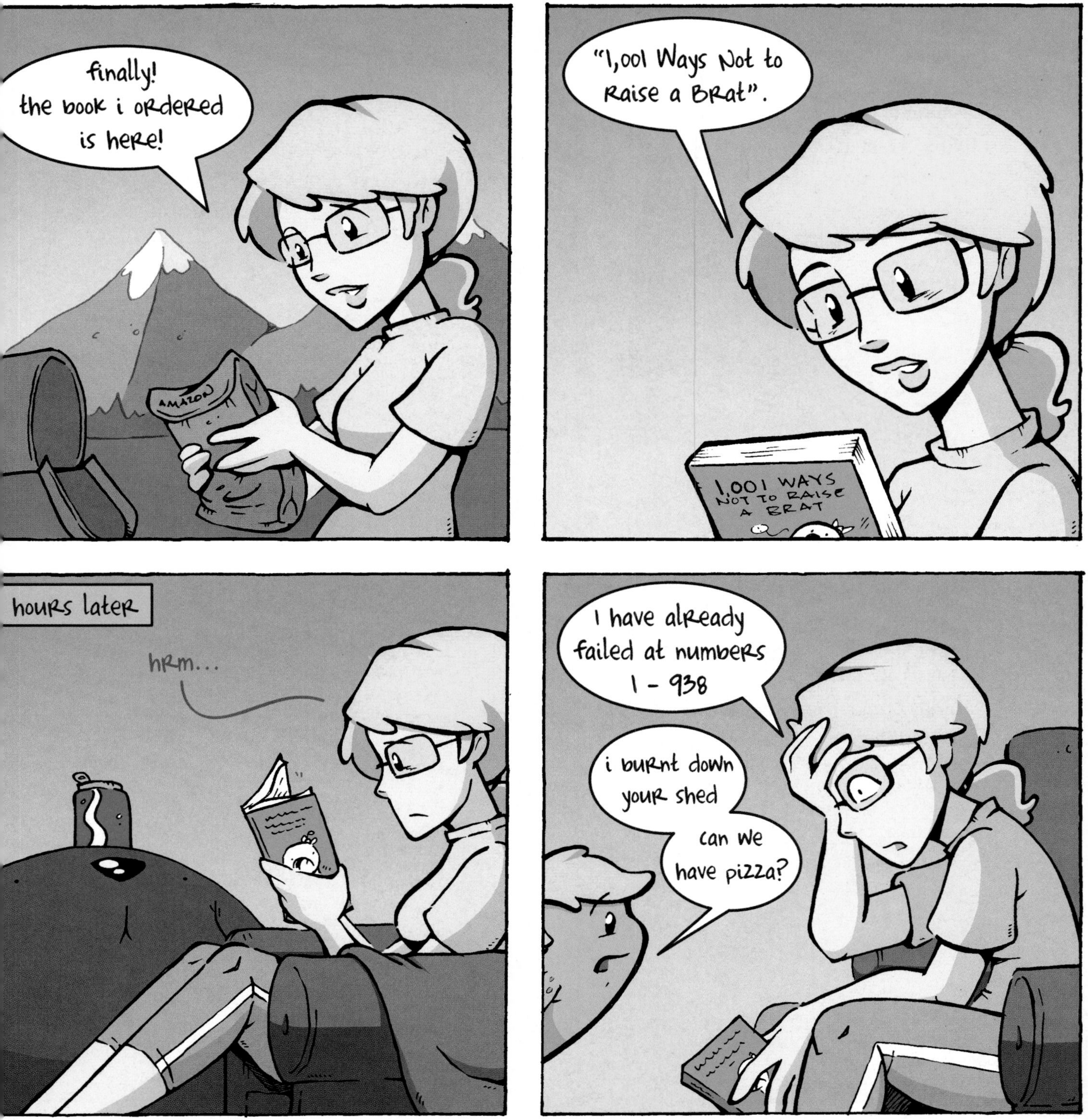
finally! the book i ordered is here!
AMAZON
"1,001 Ways Not to Raise a Brat".
1,001 WAYS NOT TO RAISE A BRAT
hours later
hrm...
I have already failed at numbers 1 - 938
i burnt down your shed
can we have pizza?

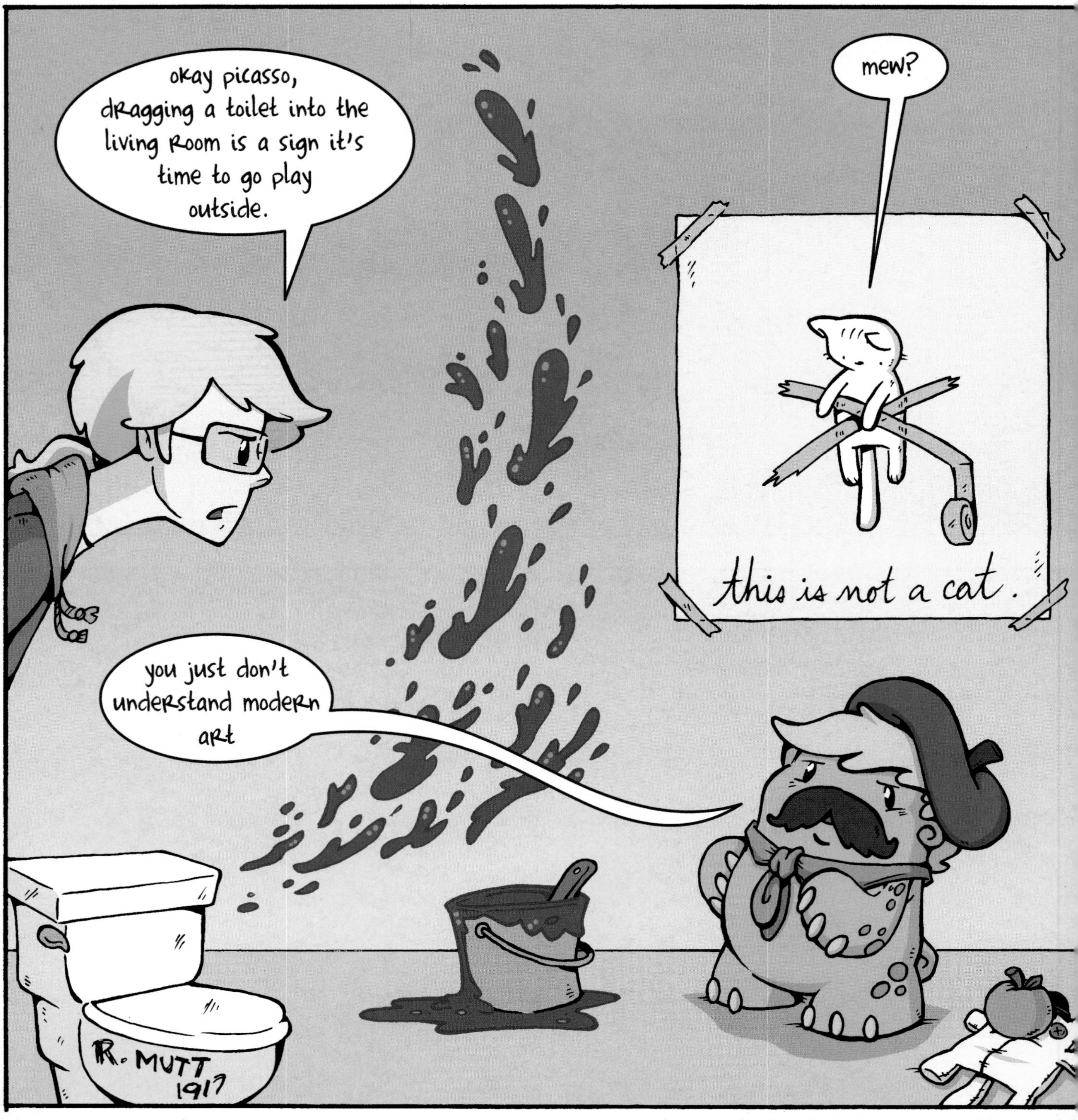
okay picasso, dragging a toilet into the living room is a sign it's time to go play outside.
mew?
this is not a cat.
you just don't understand modern art
R. MUTT 1917

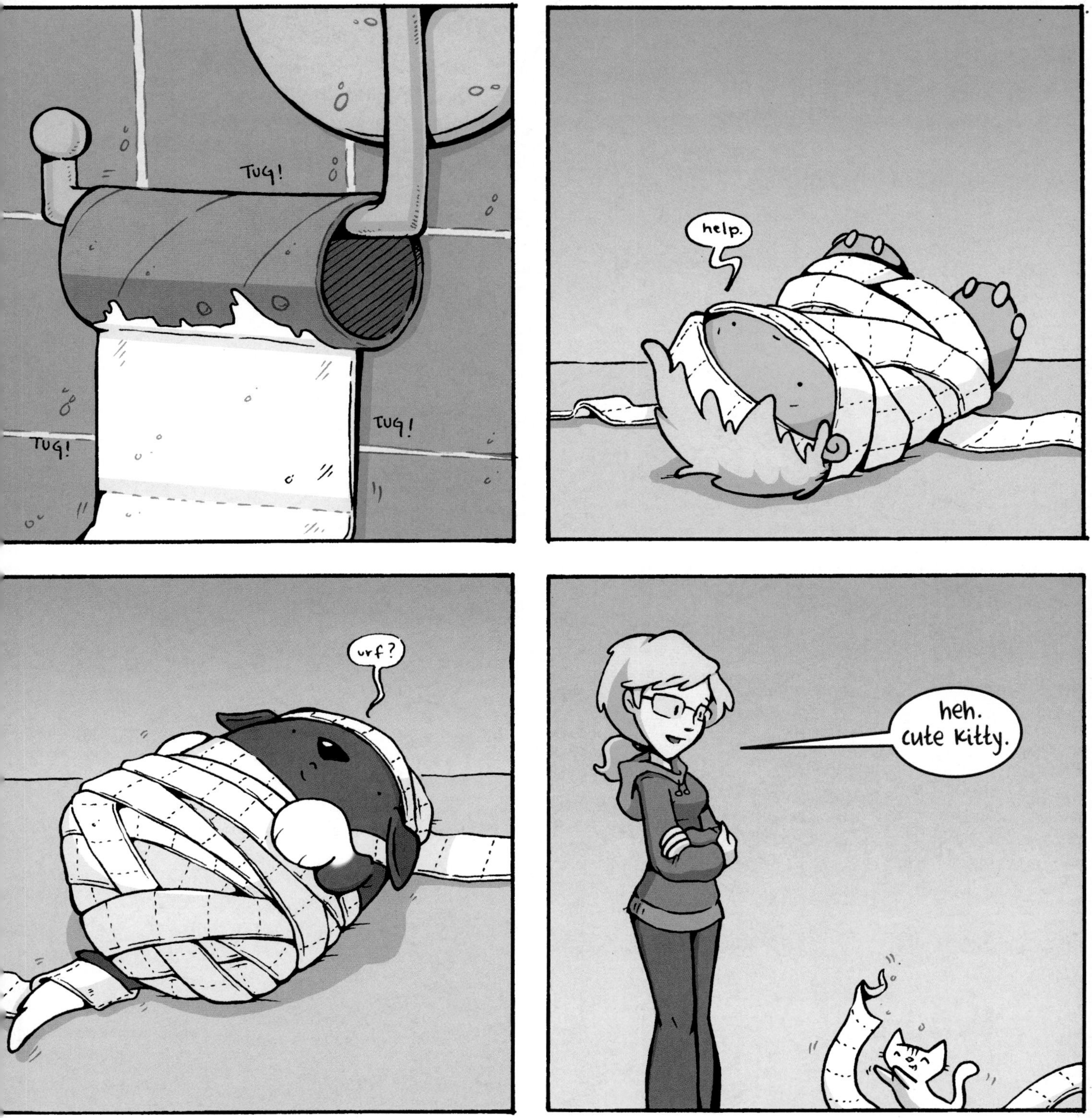
TUG!
TUG!
TUG!
help.
urf?
heh. cute kitty.

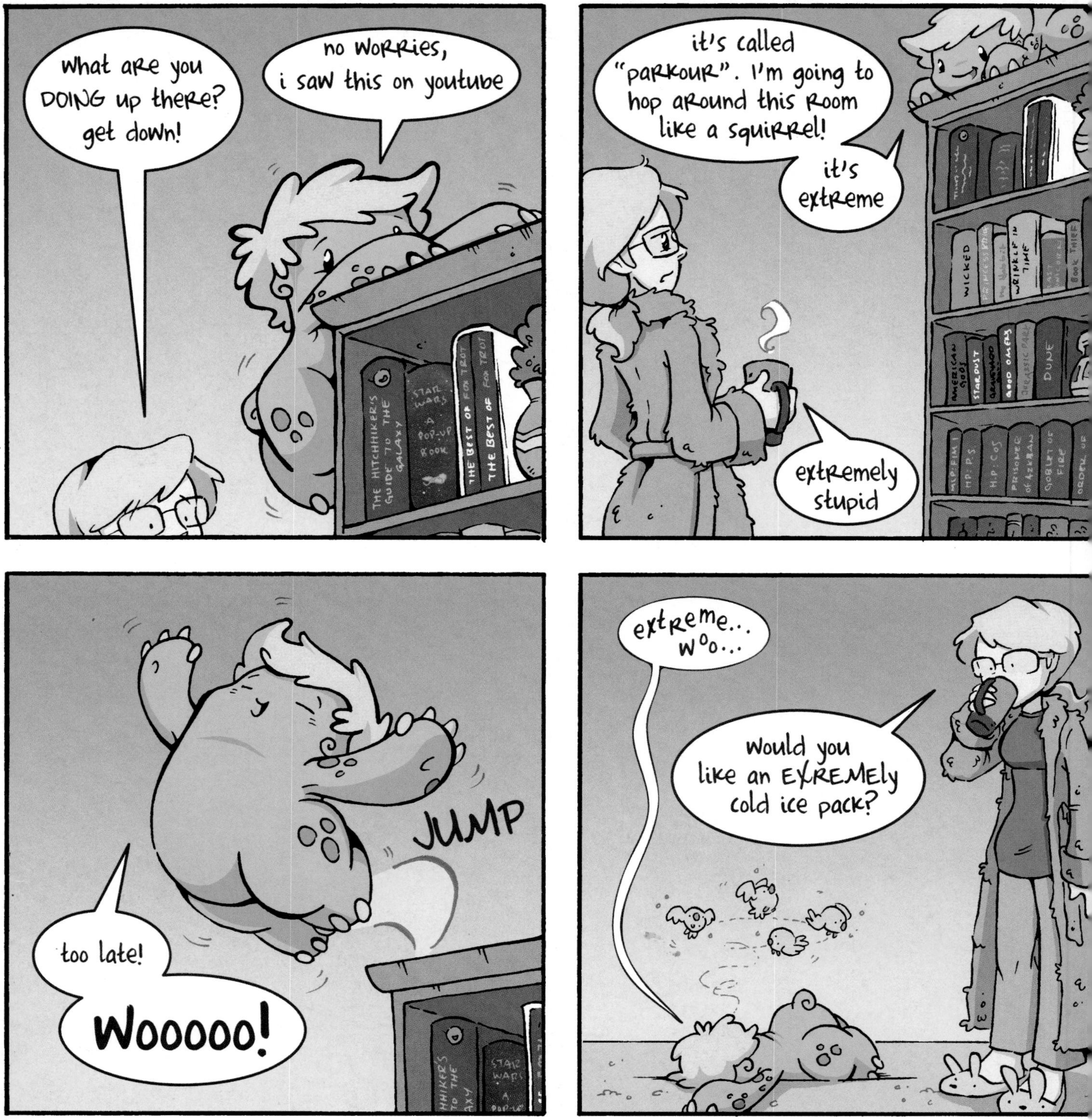
What are you DOING up there? get down!
no WoRRies, i saw this on youtube
it's called "parkour". I'm going to hop around this room like a squirrel!
it's extreme
extremely stupid
JUMP
too late!
Wooooo!
extreme... woo...
Would you like an EXREMEly cold ice pack?

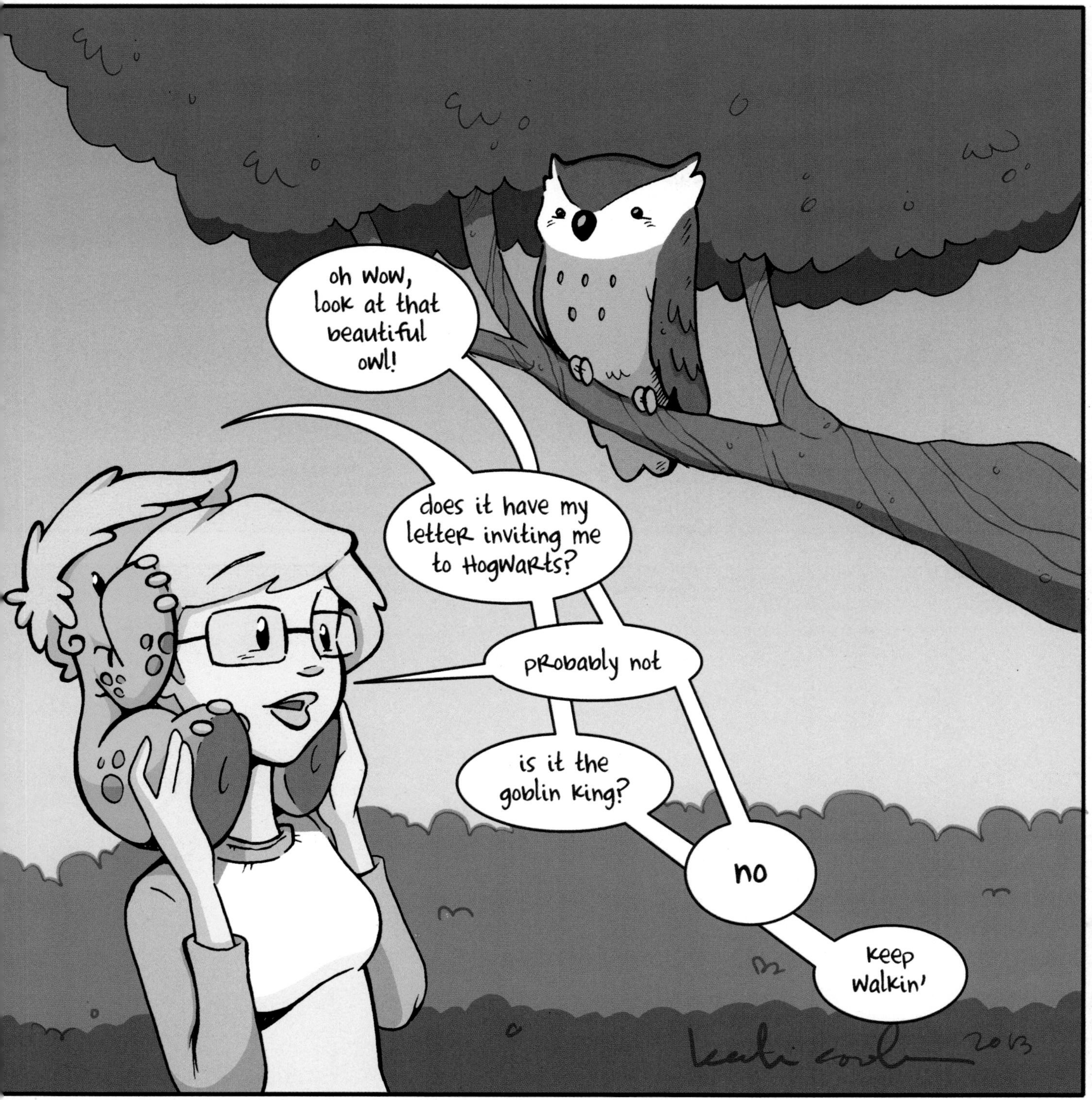
oh wow, look at that beautiful owl!
does it have my letter inviting me to Hogwarts?
probably not
is it the goblin king?
no
keep walkin'

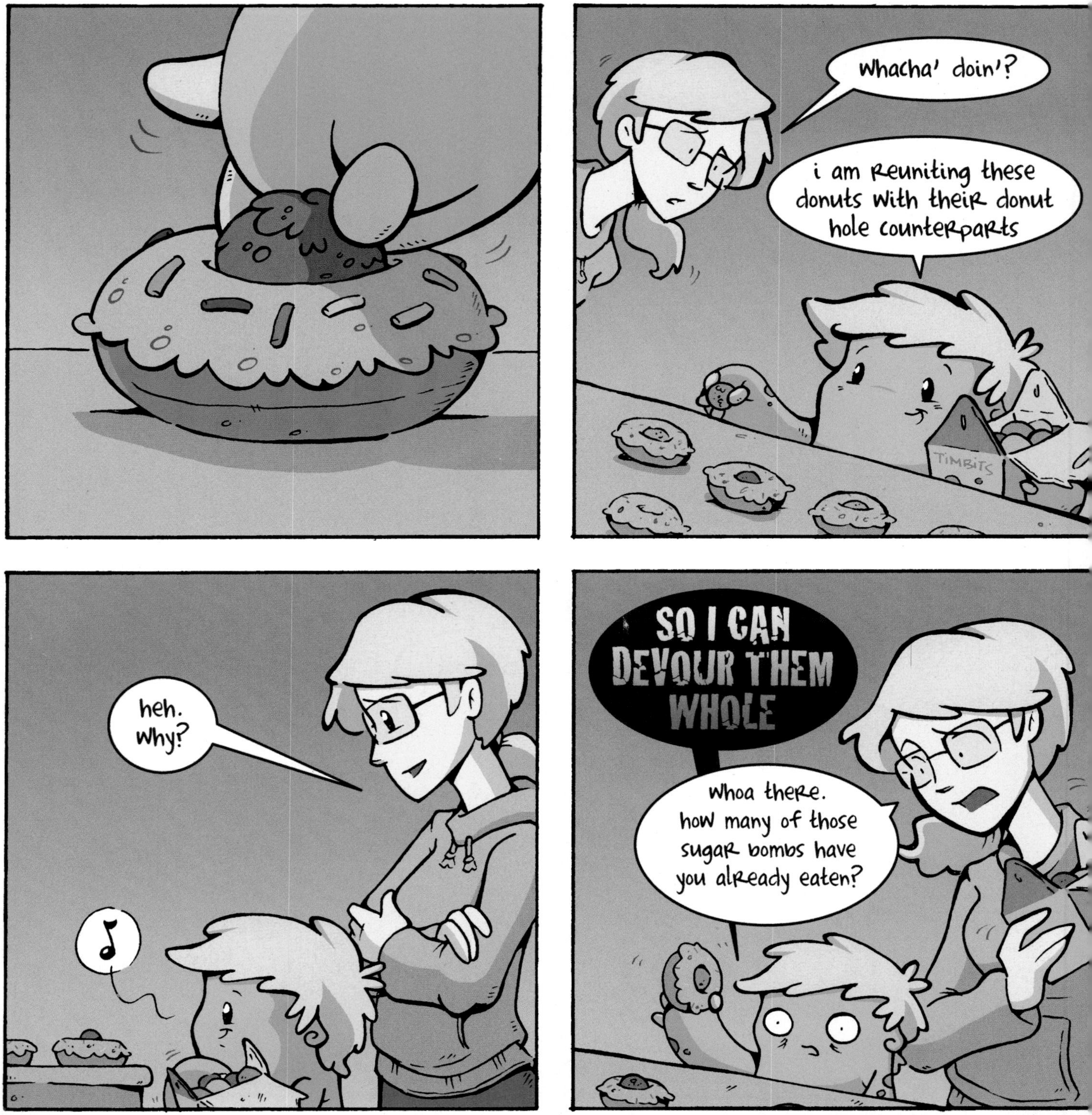
Whacha' doin'?
i am Reuniting these donuts with their donut hole counterparts
TIMBITS
heh. Why?
SO I CAN DEVOUR THEM WHOLE
Whoa there. how many of those sugar bombs have you already eaten?

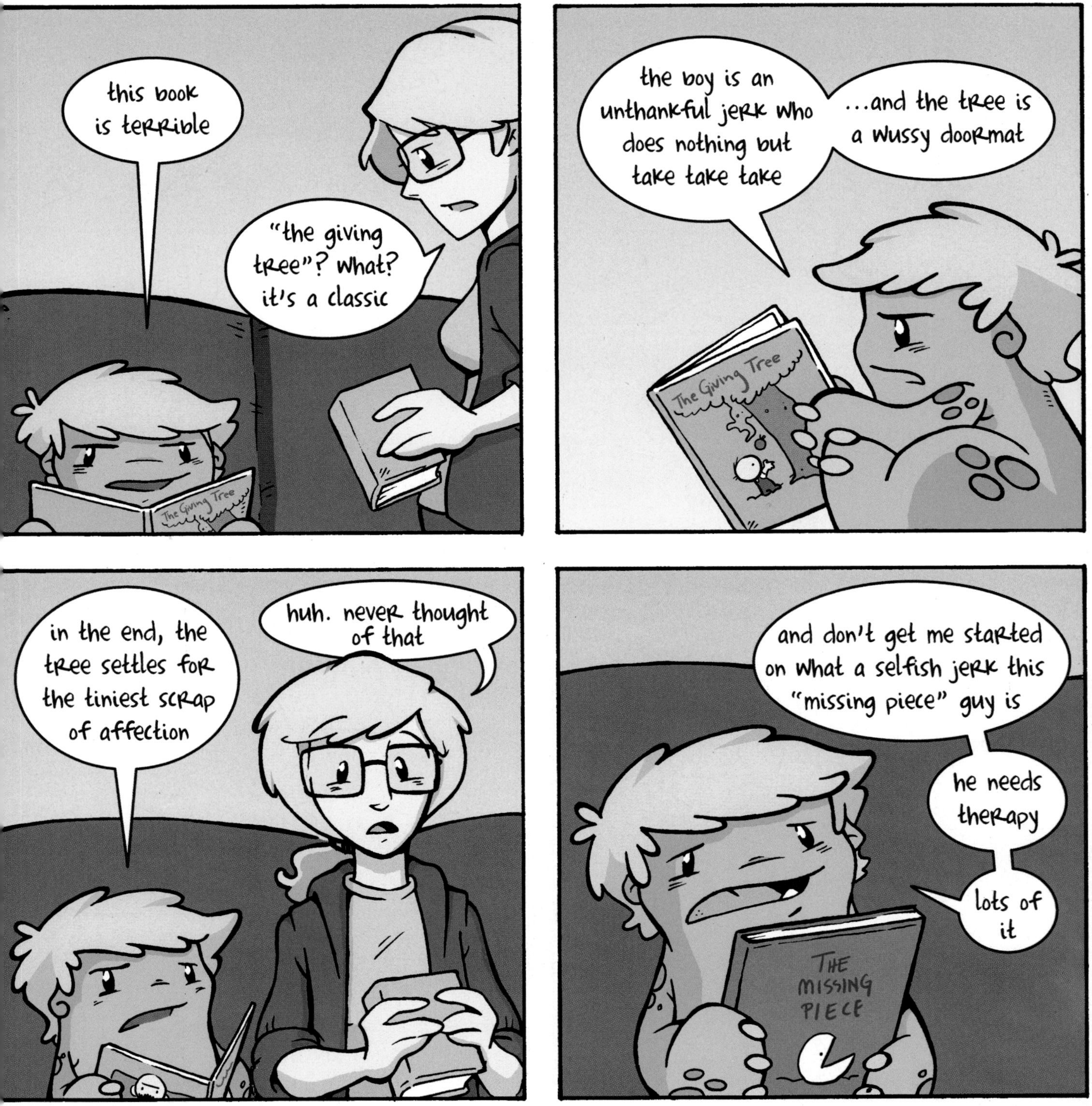

this book is terrible
"the giving tree"? what? it's a classic
The Giving Tree
the boy is an unthankful jerk who does nothing but take take take
...and the tree is a wussy doormat
The Giving Tree
in the end, the tree settles for the tiniest scrap of affection
huh. never thought of that
and don't get me started on what a selfish jerk this "missing piece" guy is
he needs therapy
lots of it
THE MISSING PIECE

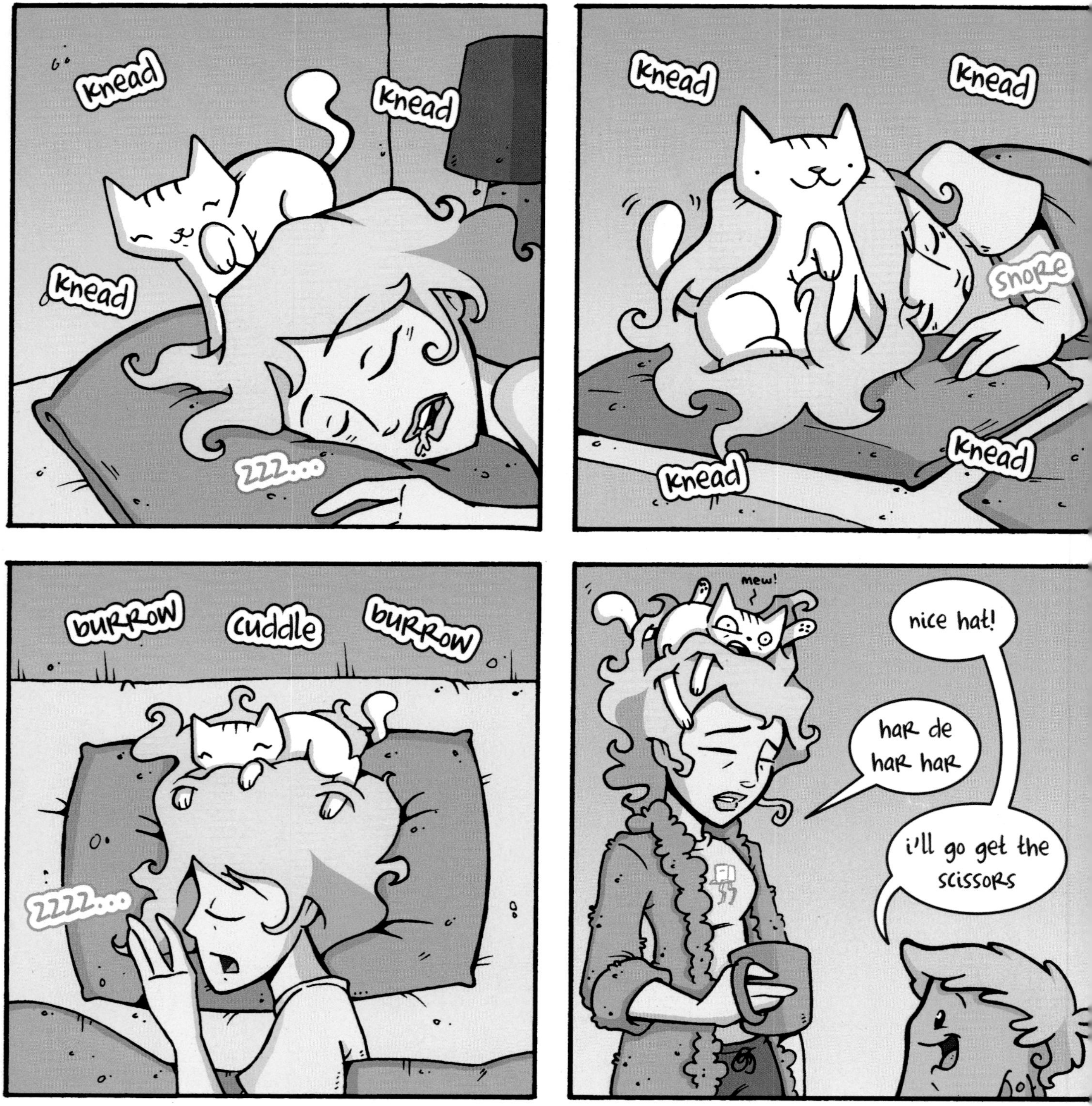
knead
knead
knead
zzz...
knead
knead
snore
knead
knead
burrow
cuddle
burrow
zzzz...
mew!
nice hat!
har de har har
i'll go get the scissors

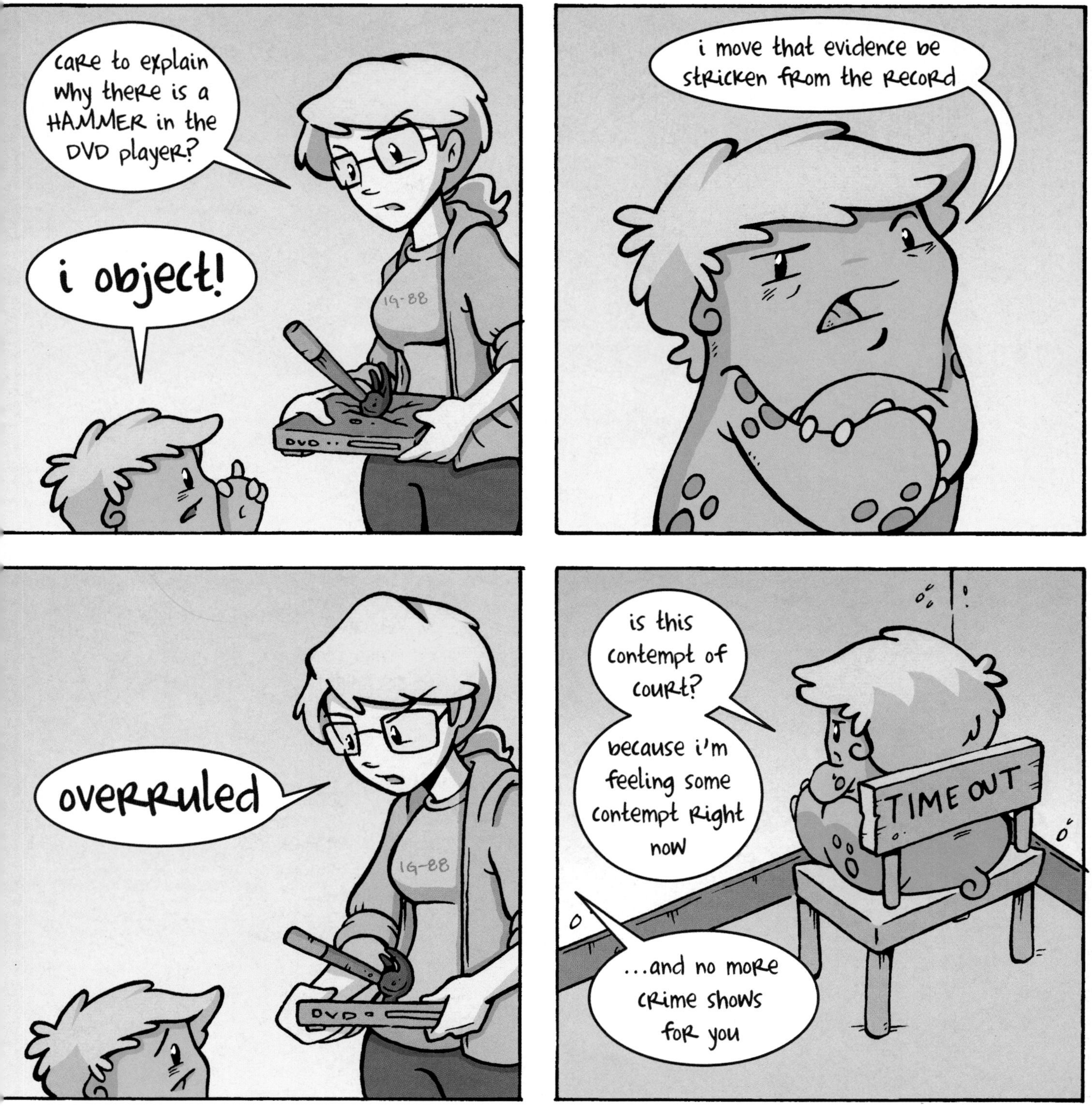
care to explain why there is a HAMMER in the DVD player?
i object!
IG-88
DVD
i move that evidence be stricken from the record
overruled
IG-88
DVD
is this contempt of court?
because i'm feeling some contempt right now
TIME OUT
...and no more crime shows for you

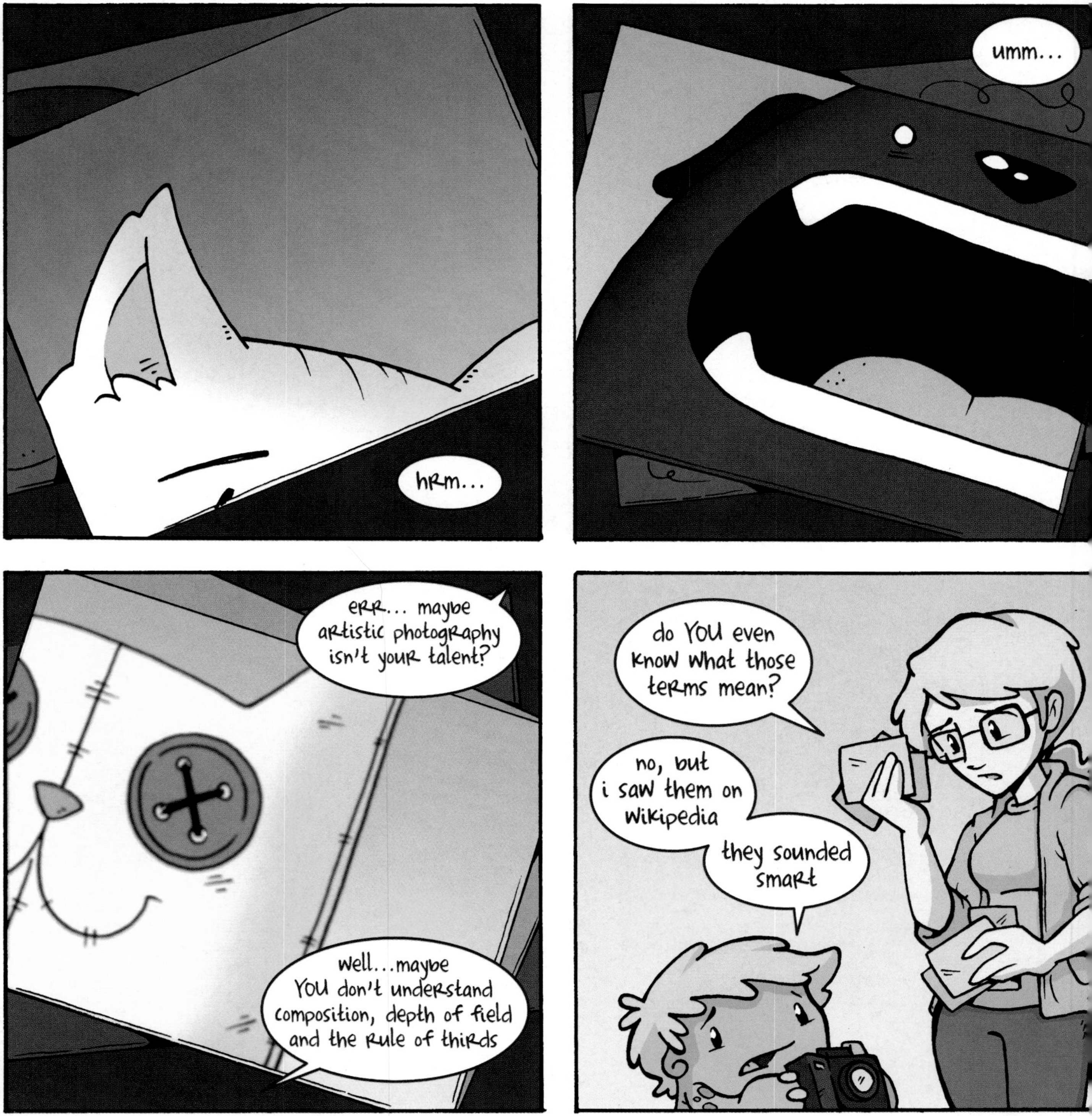
hrm...
umm...
err... maybe artistic photography isn't your talent?
well...maybe YOU don't understand composition, depth of field and the rule of thirds
do YOU even know what those terms mean?
no, but i saw them on Wikipedia
they sounded smart

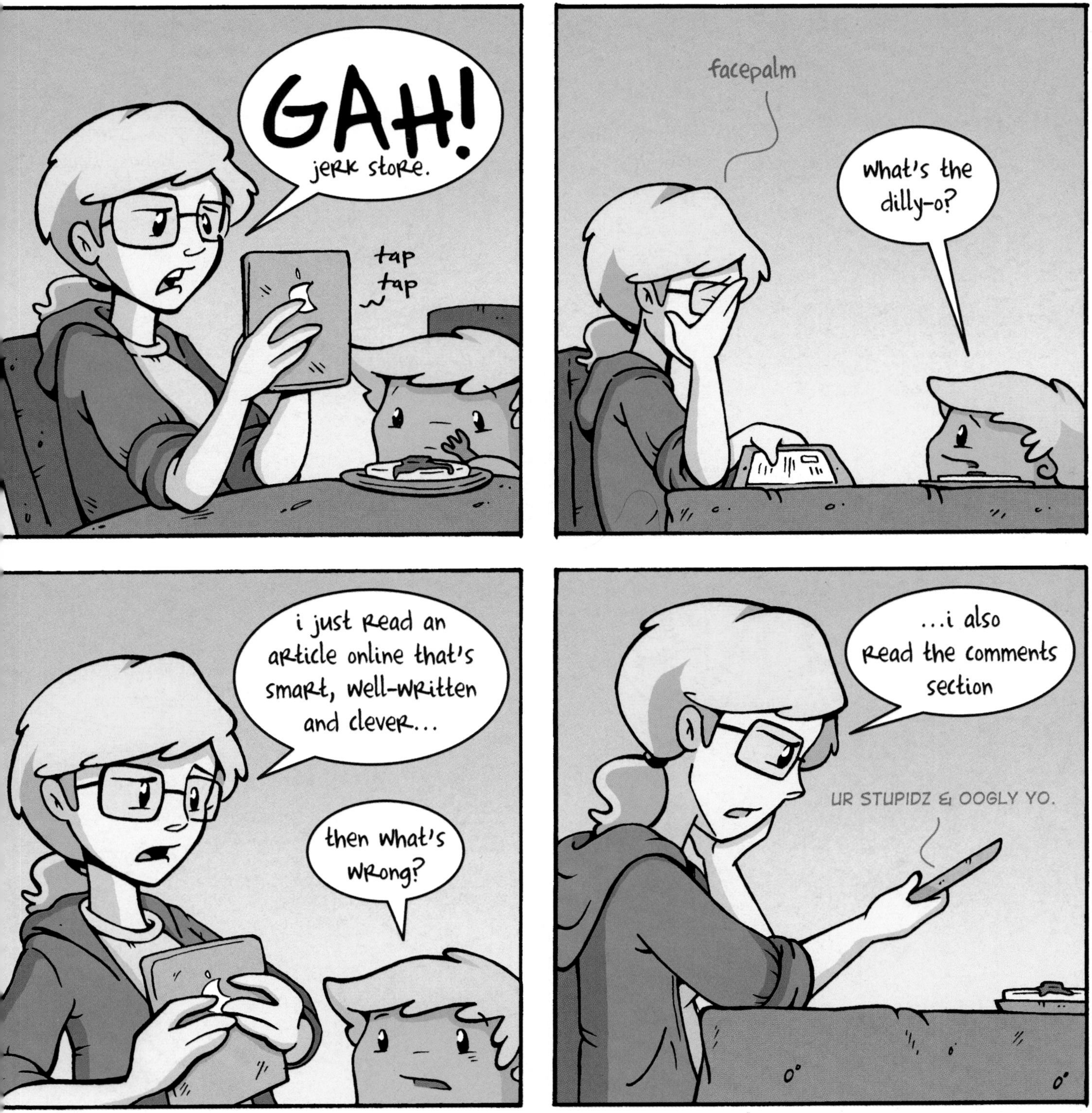
GAH!
jerk store.
tap tap
facepalm
What's the dilly-o?
i just read an article online that's smart, well-written and clever...
then what's wrong?
...i also read the comments section
UR STUPIDZ & OOGLY YO.

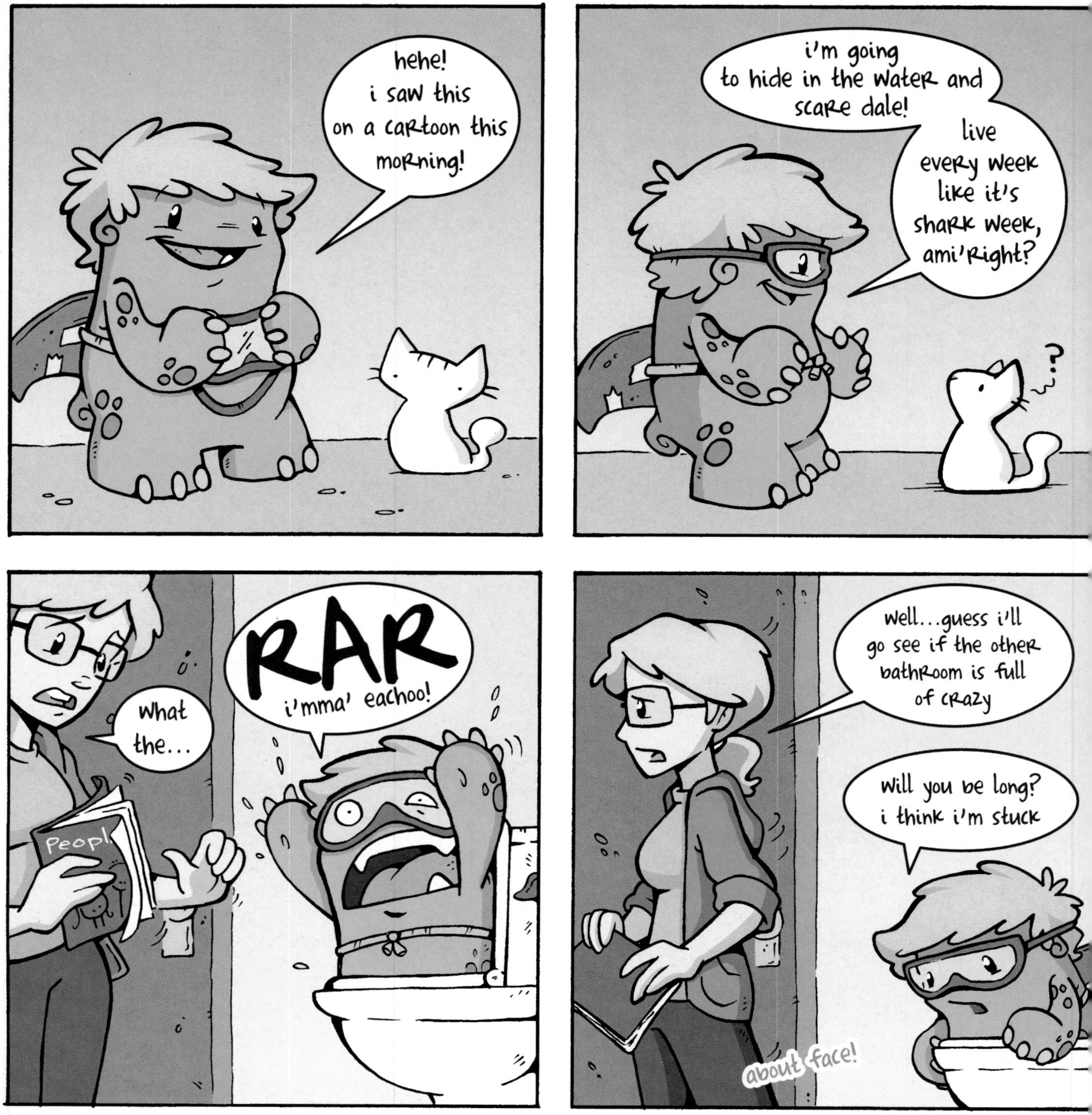
hehe! i saw this on a cartoon this morning!
i'm going to hide in the water and scare dale!
live every week like it's shark week, ami'right?
?
What the...
RAR i'mma' eachoo!
well...guess i'll go see if the other bathroom is full of crazy
about face!
will you be long? i think i'm stuck
Peopl

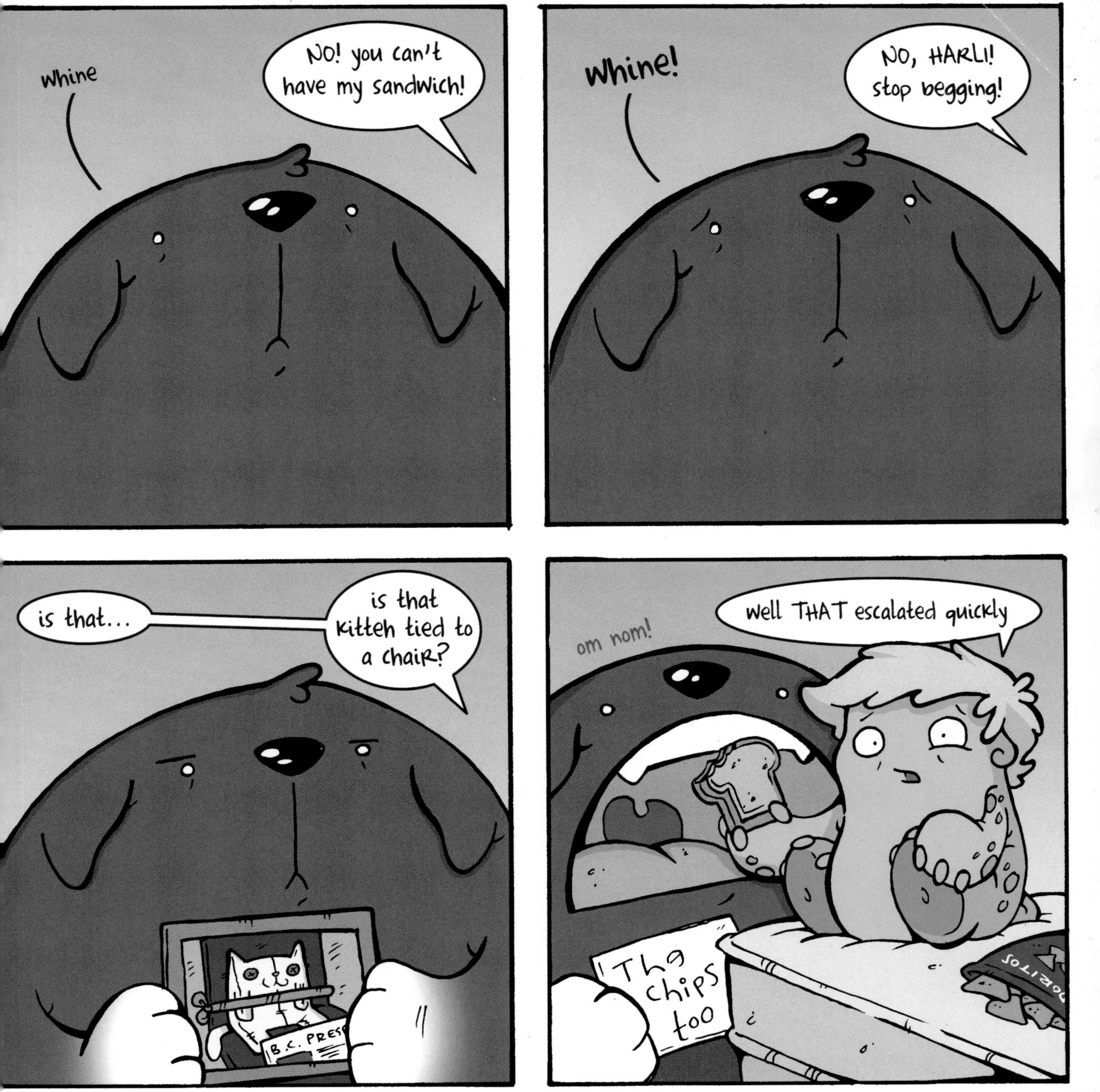
whine
NO! you can't have my sandwich!
Whine!
NO, HARLI! stop begging!
is that...
is that kitteh tied to a chair?
B.C. PRES
om nom!
well THAT escalated quickly
Tha chips too
DORITOS

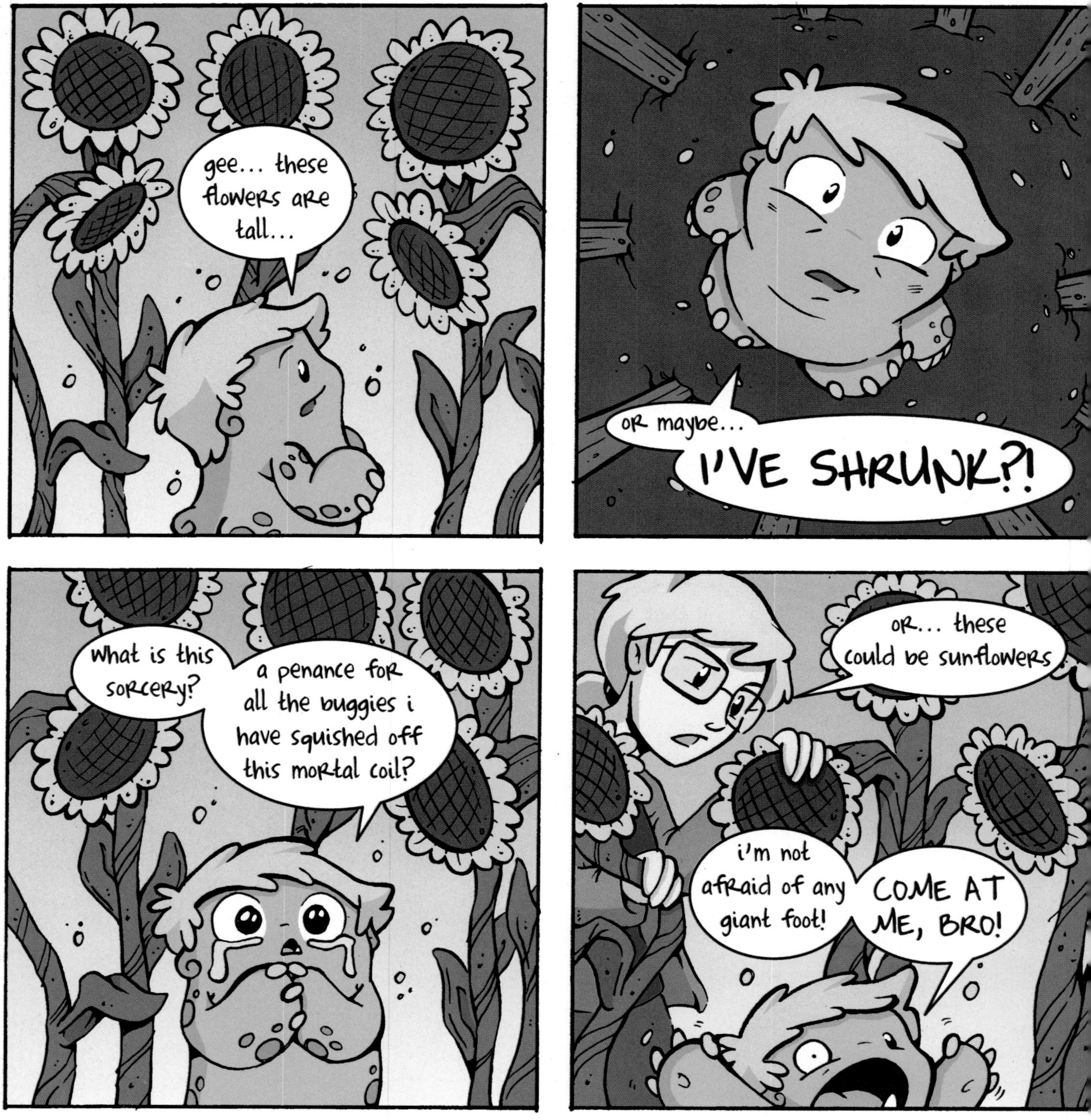
gee... these flowers are tall...
or maybe...
I'VE SHRUNK?!
What is this sorcery?
a penance for all the buggies i have squished off this mortal coil?
or... these could be sunflowers
i'm not afraid of any giant foot!
COME AT ME, BRO!

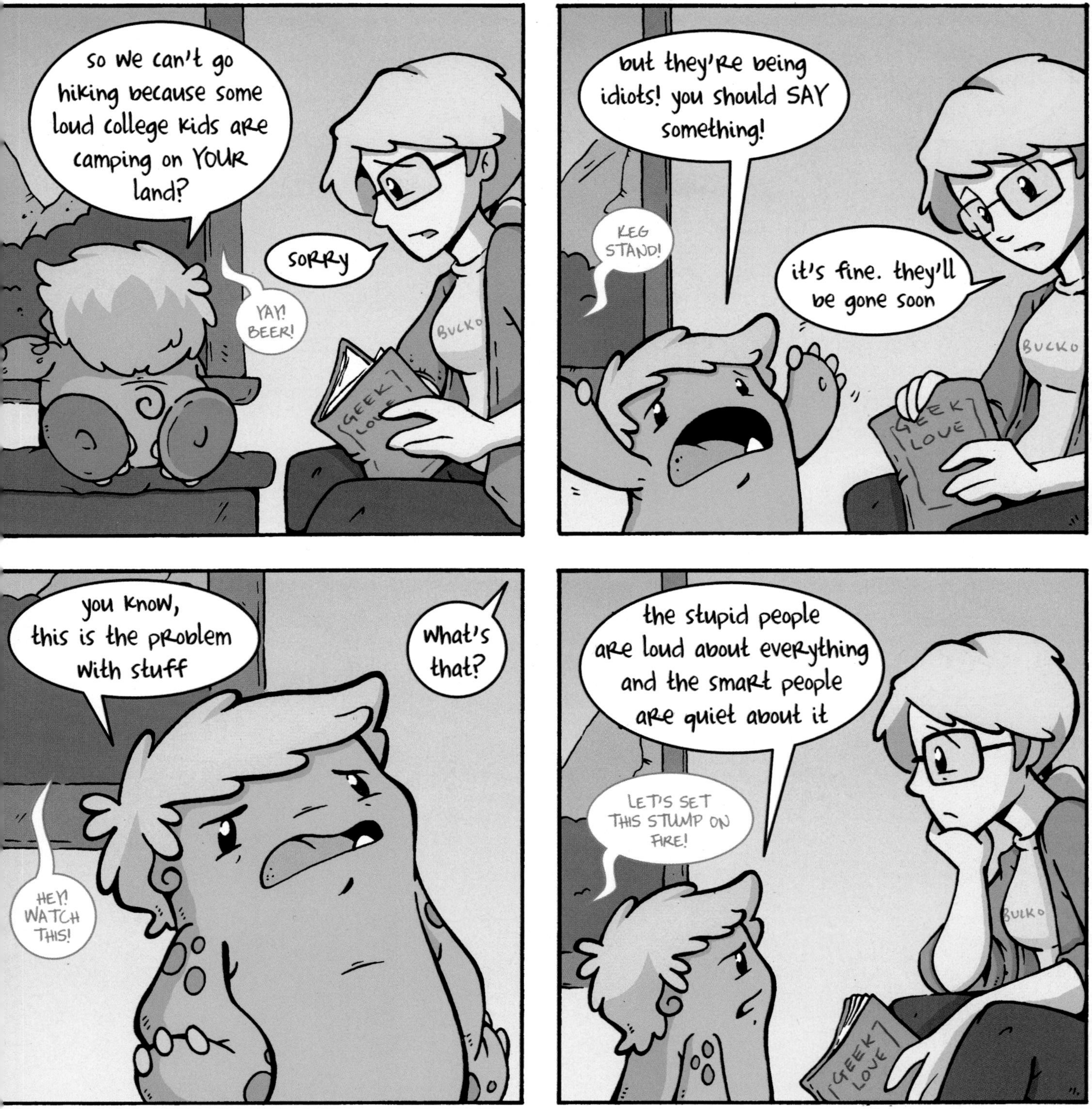
so we can't go hiking because some loud college kids are camping on YOUR land?
YAY! BEER!
sorry
but they're being idiots! you should SAY something!
KEG STAND!
it's fine. they'll be gone soon
you know, this is the problem with stuff
What's that?
HEY! WATCH THIS!
the stupid people are loud about everything and the smart people are quiet about it
LET'S SET THIS STUMP ON FIRE!

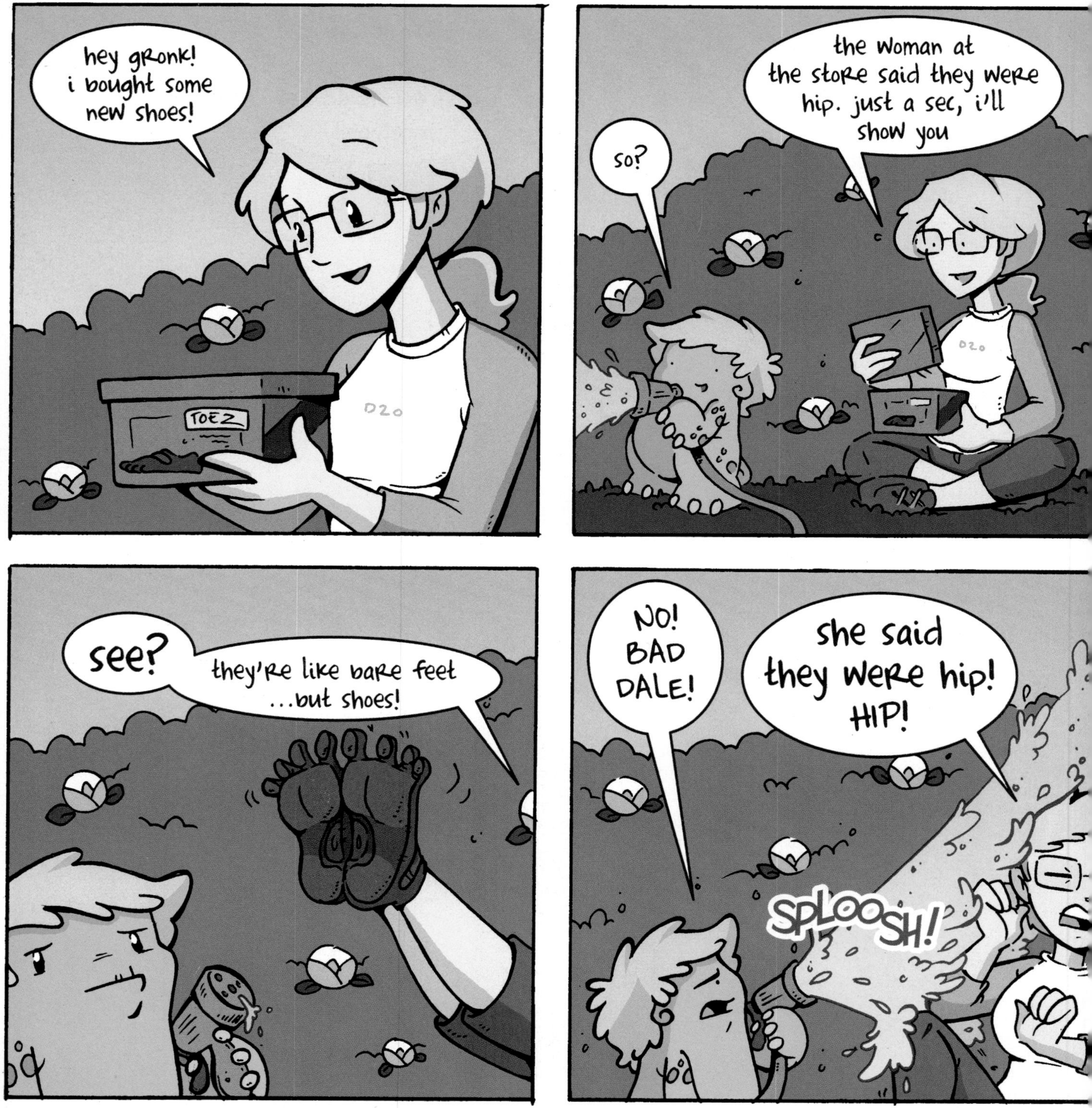
hey gronk! i bought some new shoes!
TOEZ
D2O
so?
the woman at the store said they were hip. just a sec, i'll show you
see?
they're like bare feet ...but shoes!
NO! BAD DALE!
she said they were hip! HIP!
SPLOOSH!

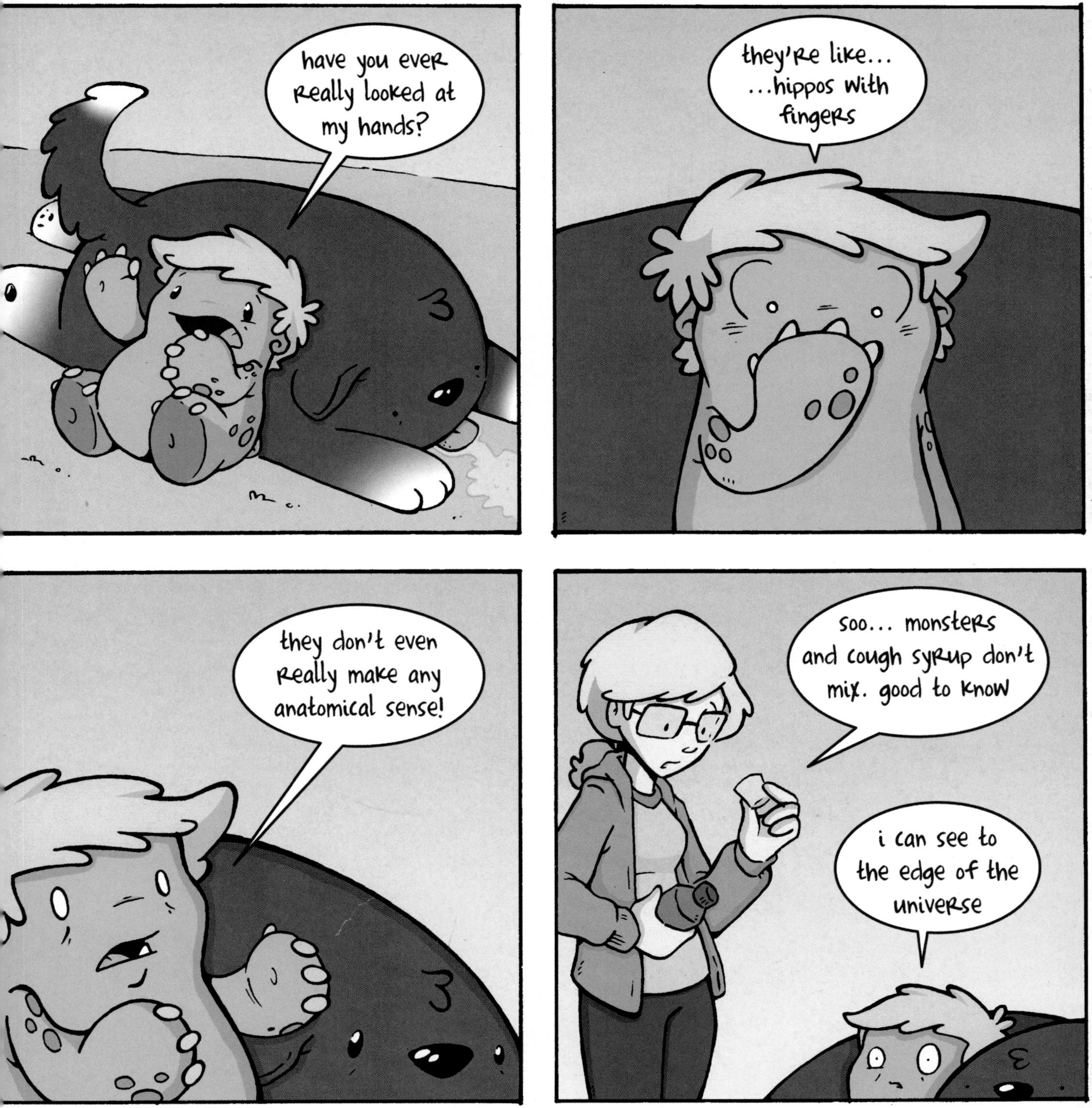
have you ever really looked at my hands?
they're like... ...hippos with fingers
they don't even really make any anatomical sense!
soo... monsters and cough syrup don't mix. good to know
i can see to the edge of the universe

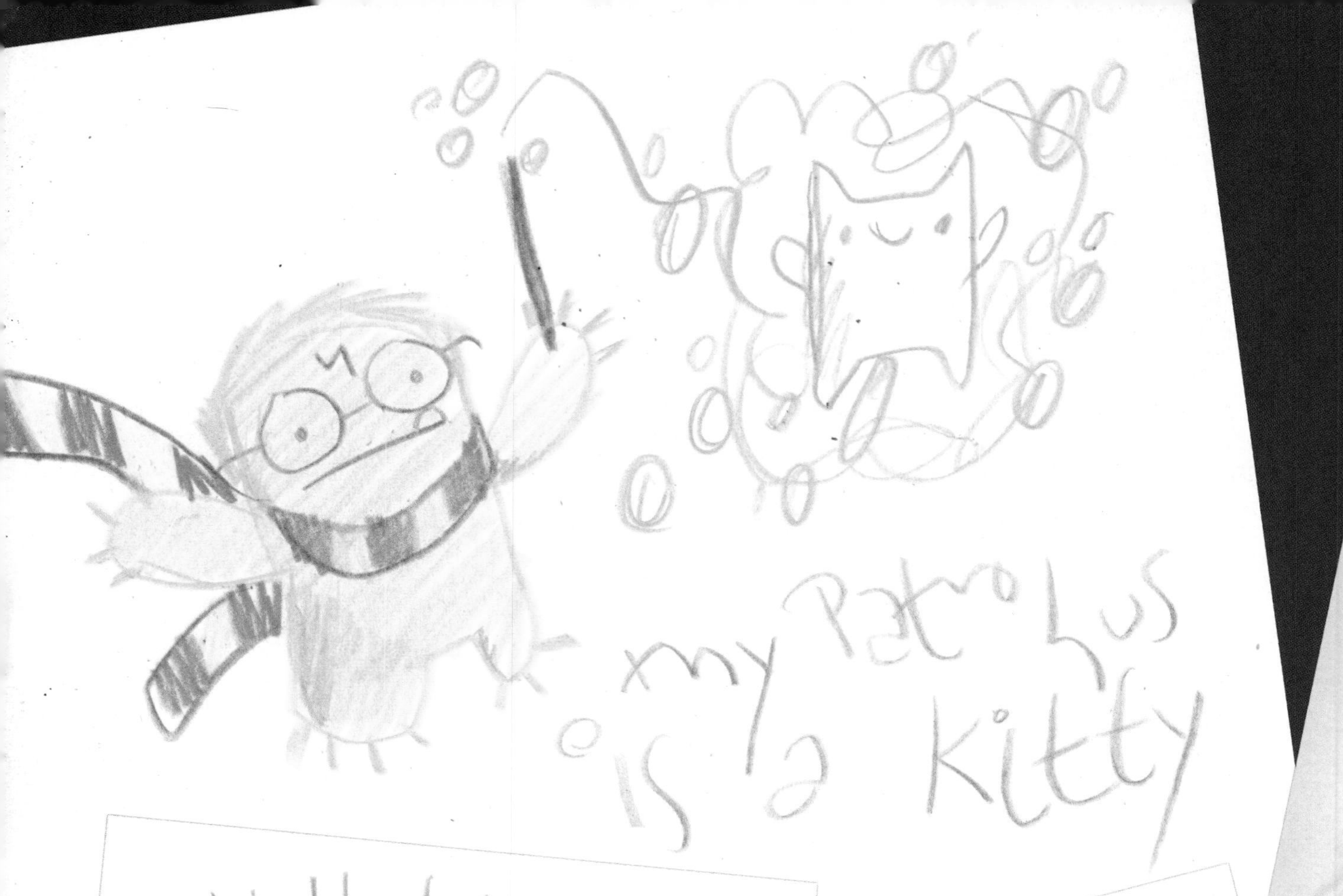
my Patronus is a kitty

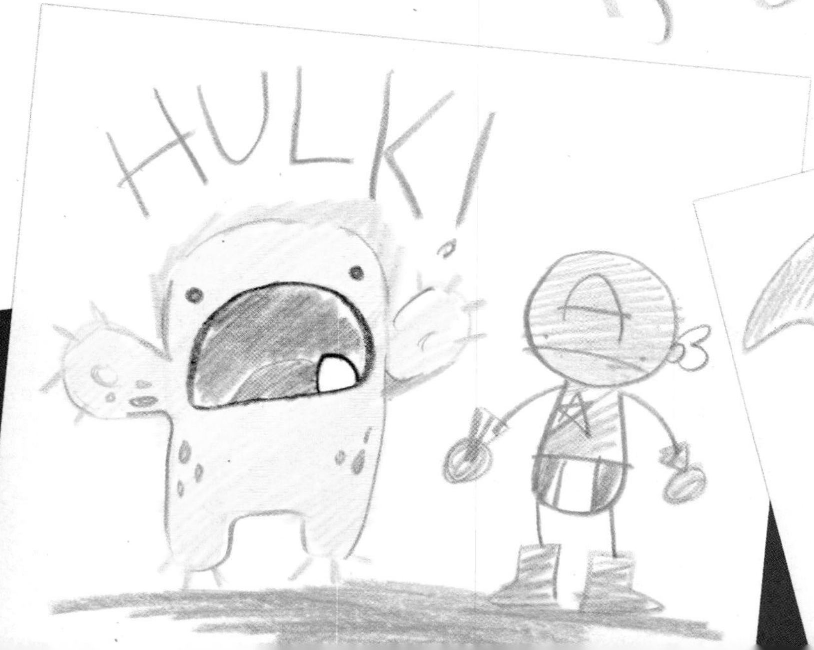
HULK!

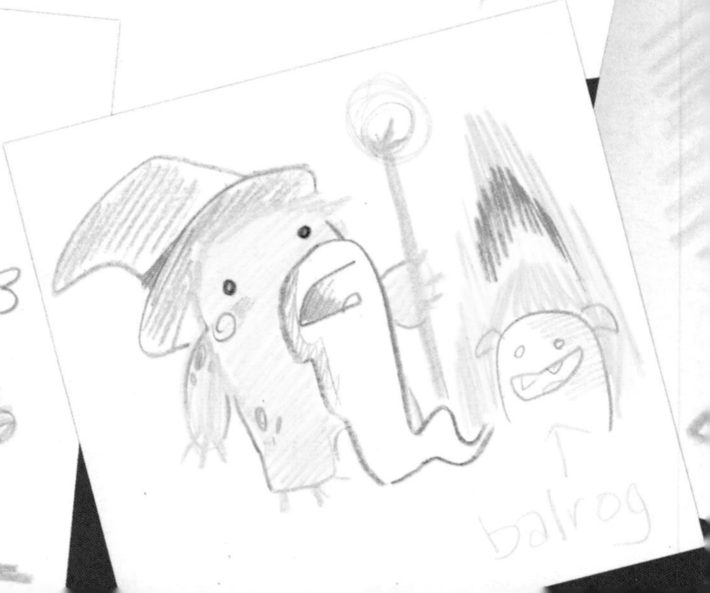
balrog

currently on Dale's fridge

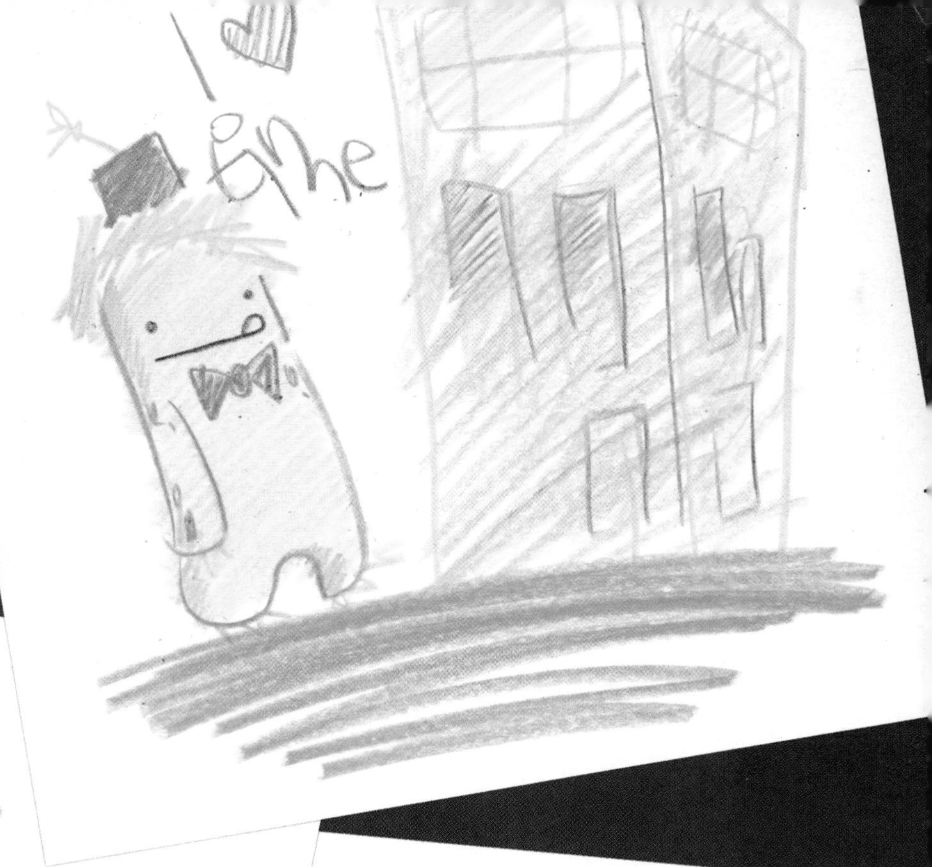
I ♥ time

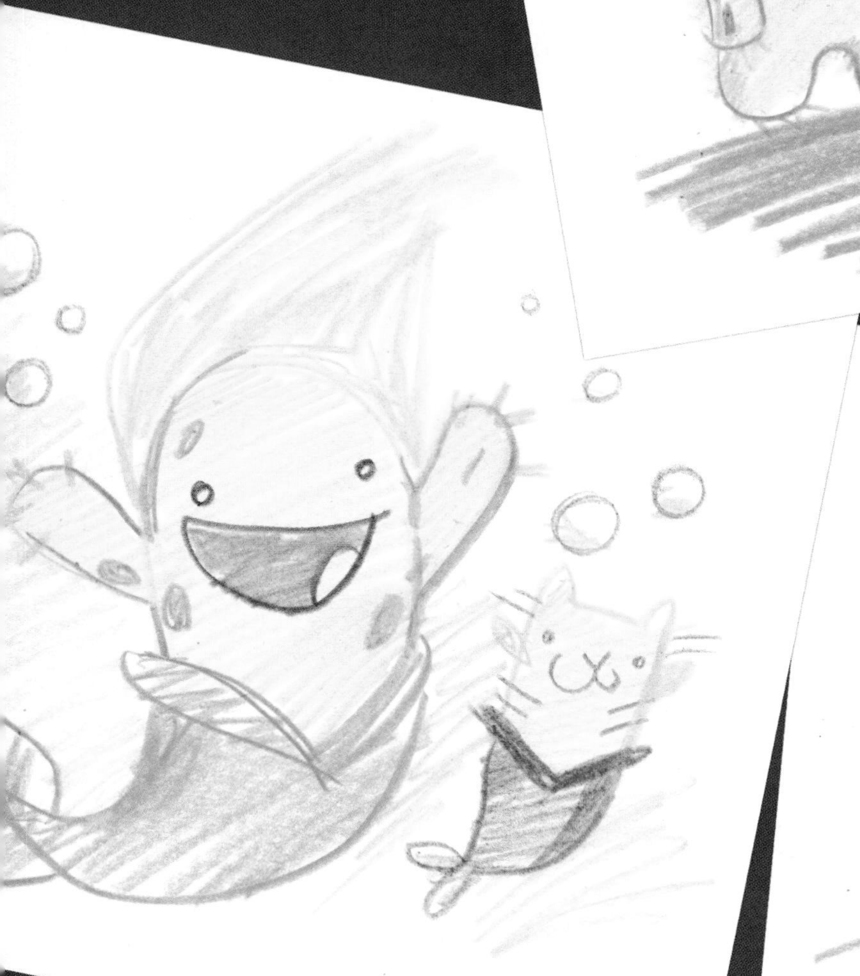

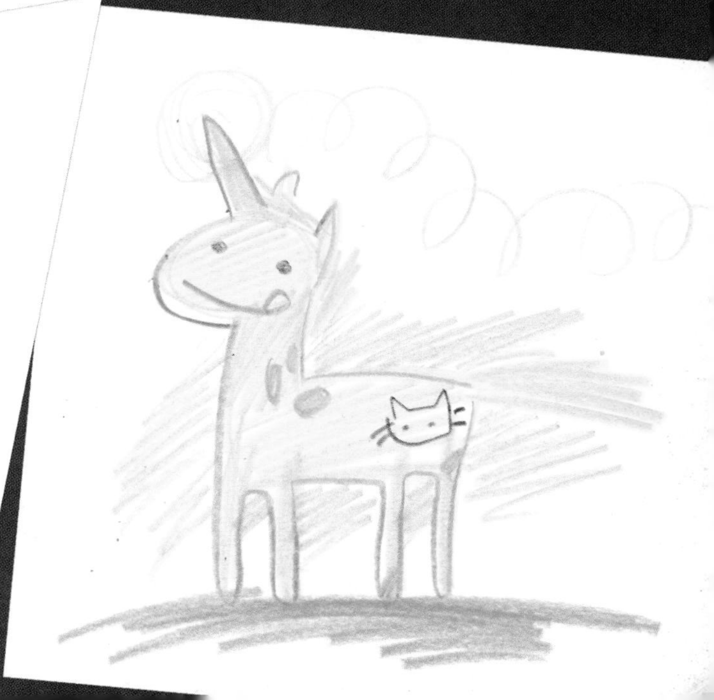

art by adam withers

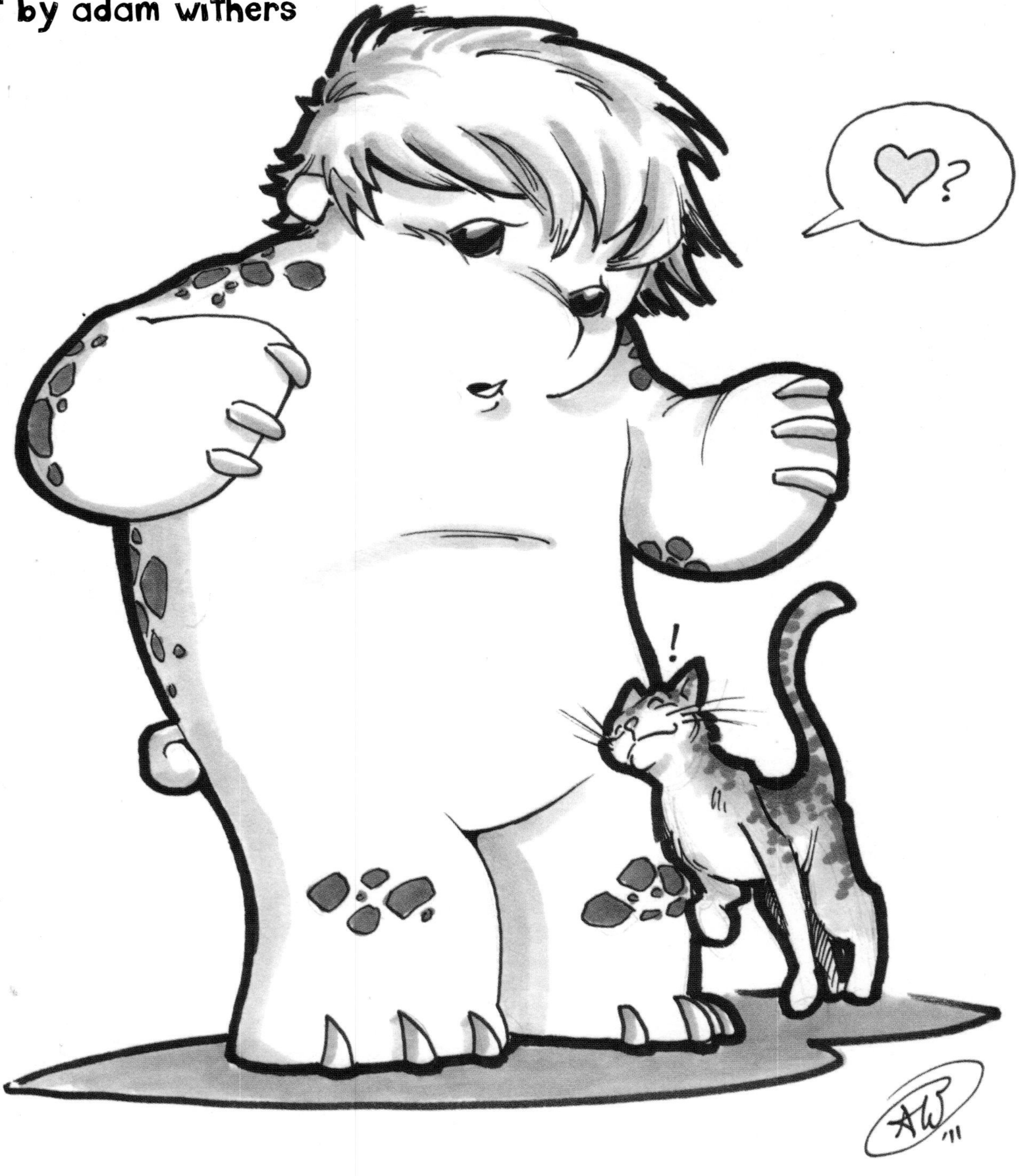

?
!
AW '11

art by denver brubaker

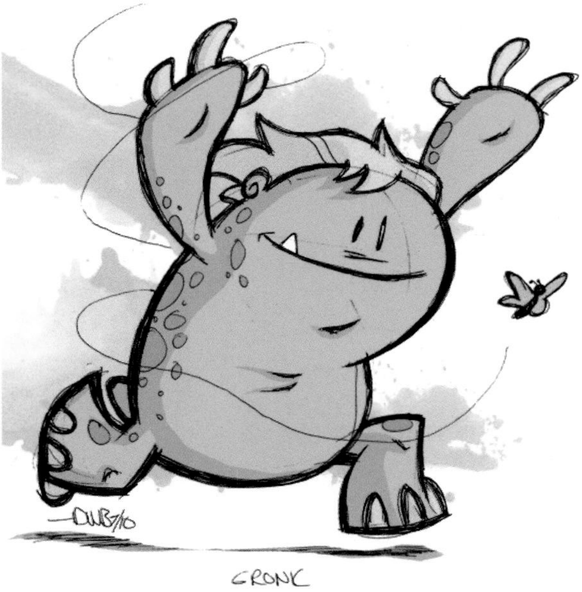
DWB/10
GRONK

art by daniel mead

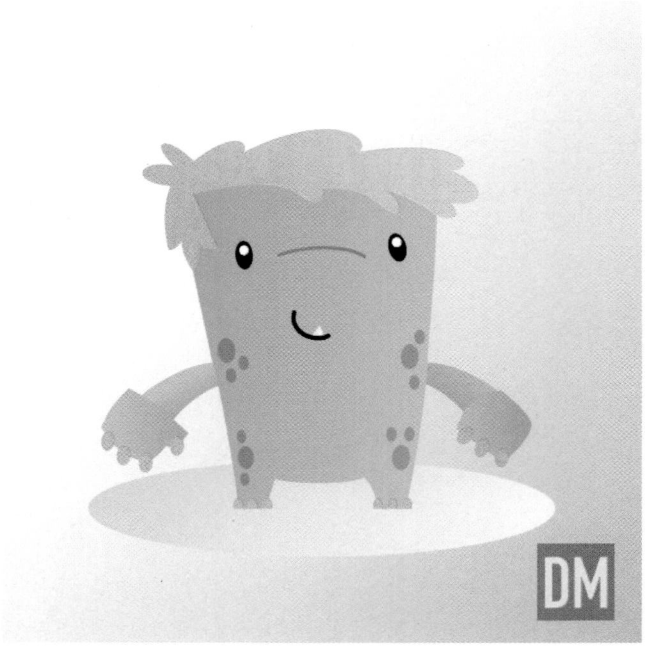
DM

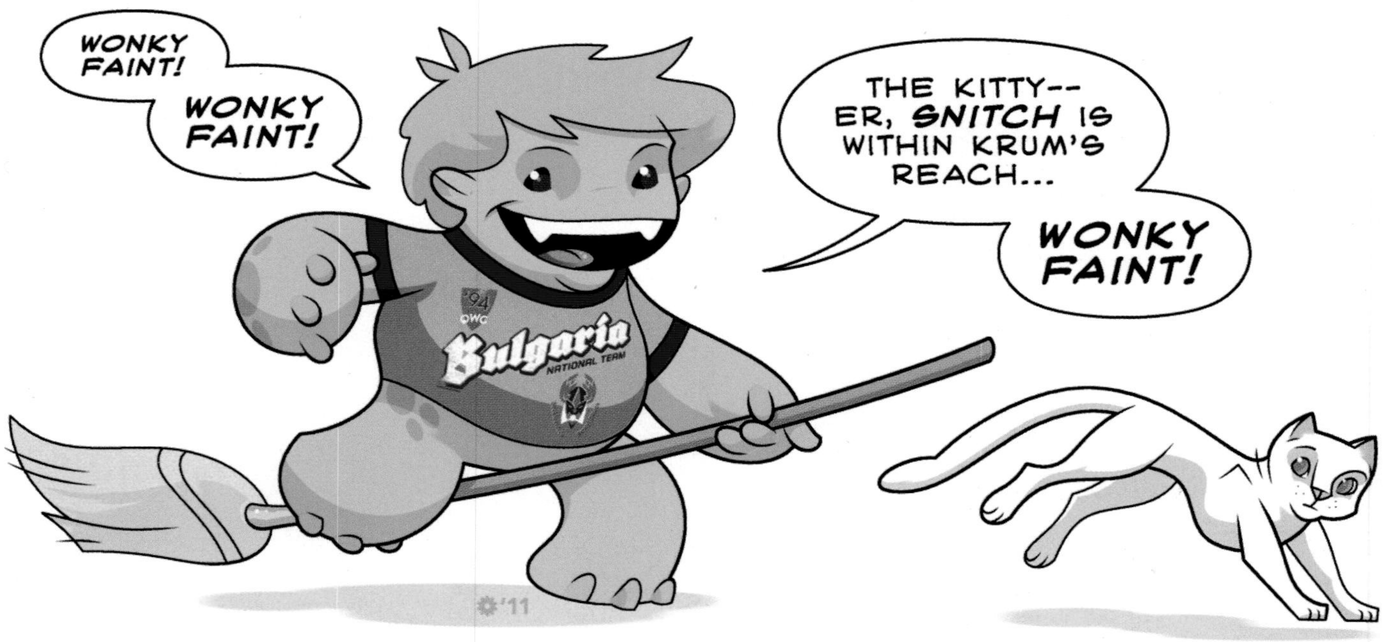
WONKY FAINT!
WONKY FAINT!
THE KITTY-- ER, SNITCH IS WITHIN KRUM'S REACH...
WONKY FAINT!
Bulgaria
NATIONAL TEAM
'94 QWC
'11

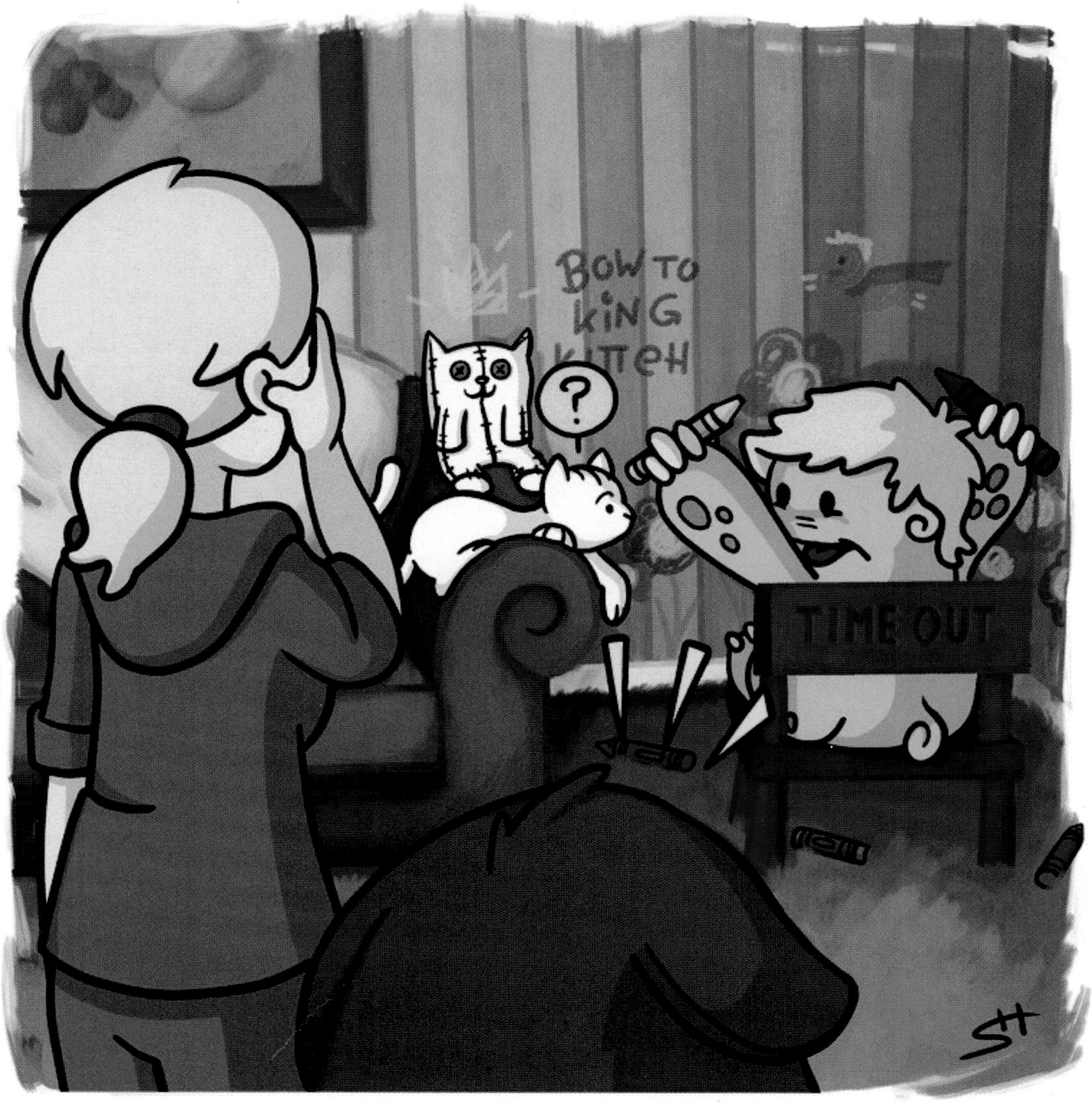
BOW TO
KING
KITTEH
?
TIME OUT

art by courtney hahn

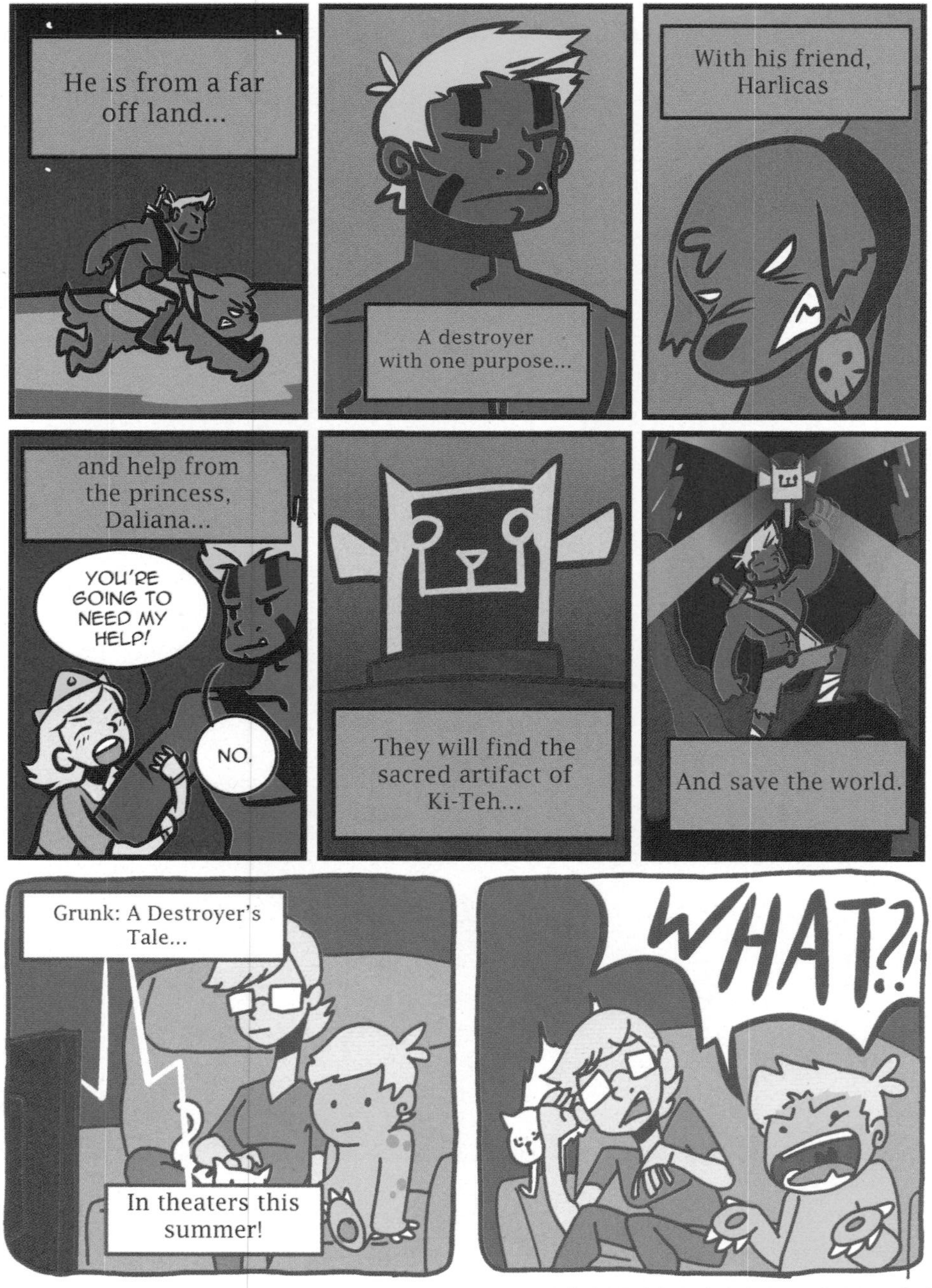
He is from a far off land...
A destroyer with one purpose...
With his friend, Harlicas
and help from the princess, Daliana...
YOU'RE GOING TO NEED MY HELP!
NO.
They will find the sacred artifact of Ki-Teh...
And save the world.
Grunk: A Destroyer's Tale...
In theaters this summer!
WHAT?!

COURTNEYHAHN.BRUSHD.COM

art by jay fosgitt

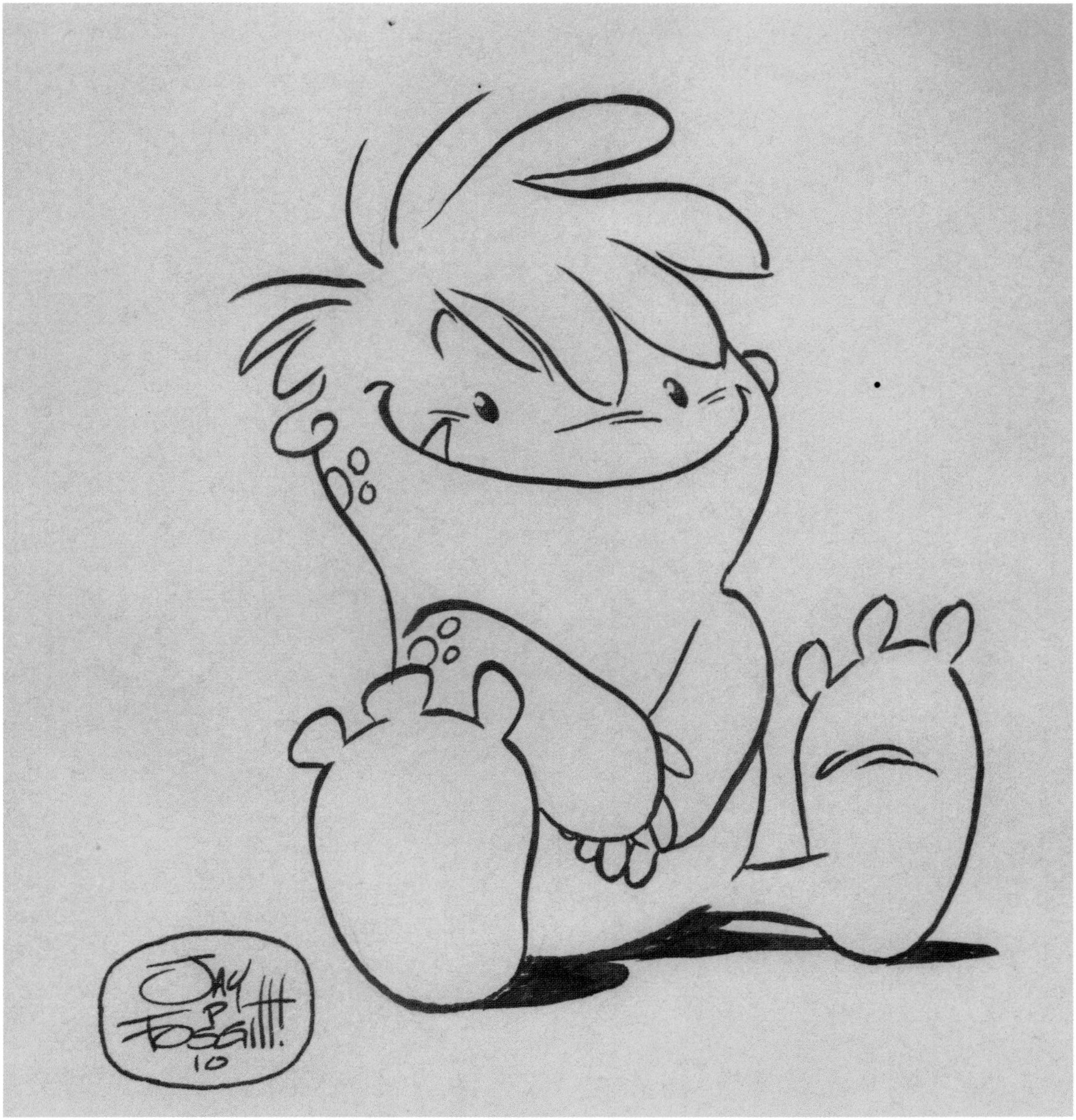

art by isabel talsma

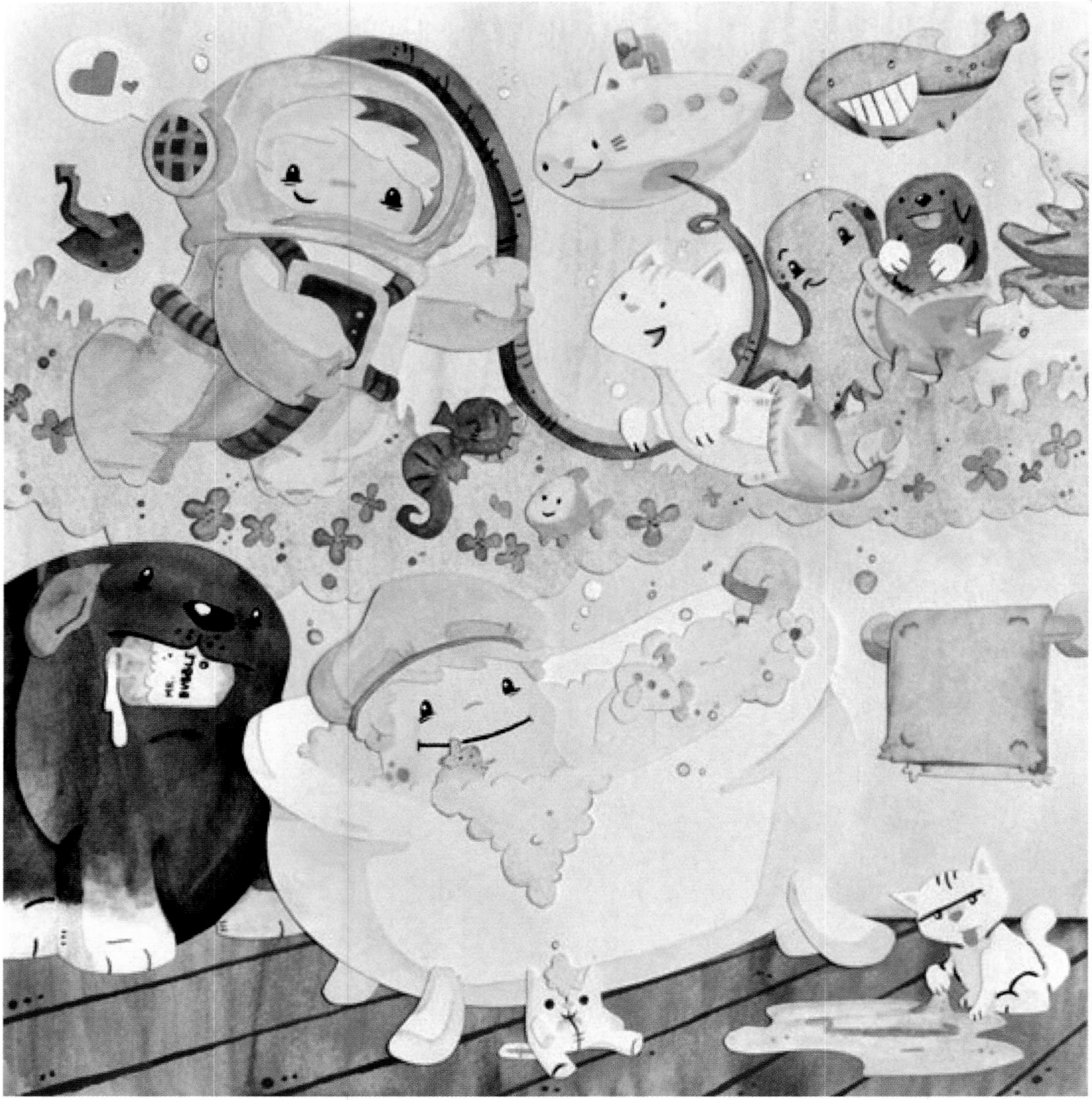

from my own sketchbook...

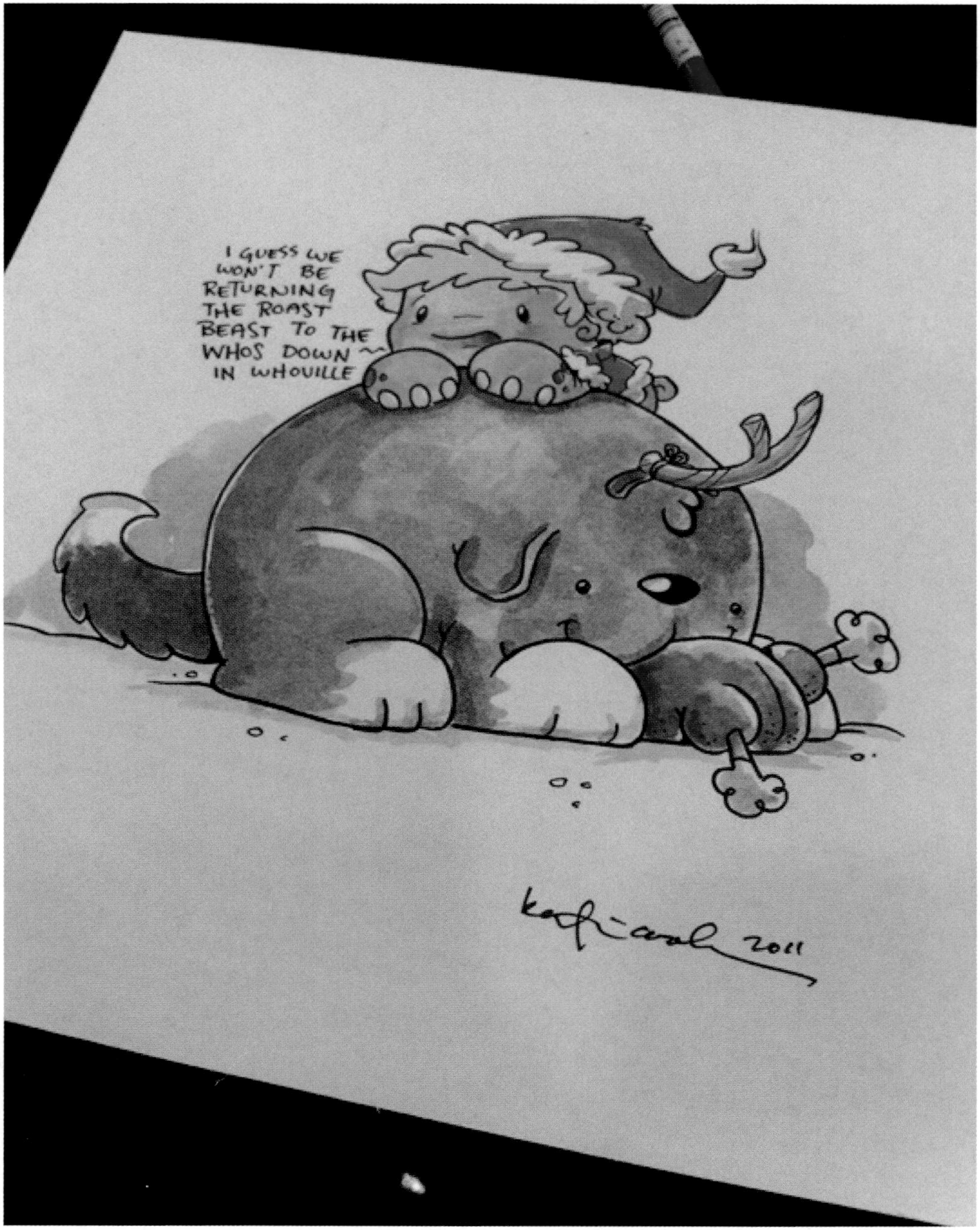
I GUESS WE WON'T BE RETURNING THE ROAST BEAST TO THE WHOS DOWN IN WHOUILLE ~
2011

gronk sculptures by katie

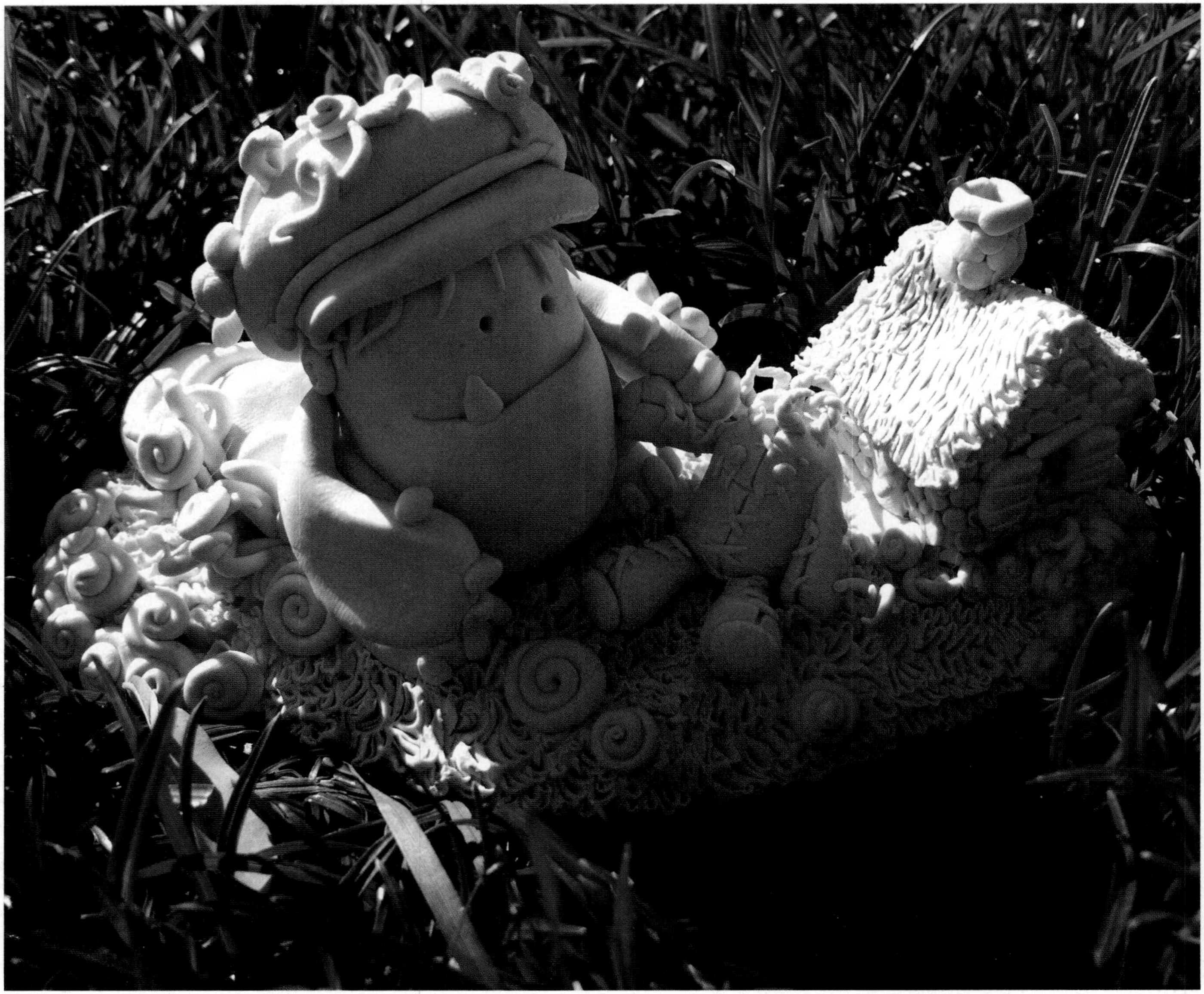

gronk sculptures by katie

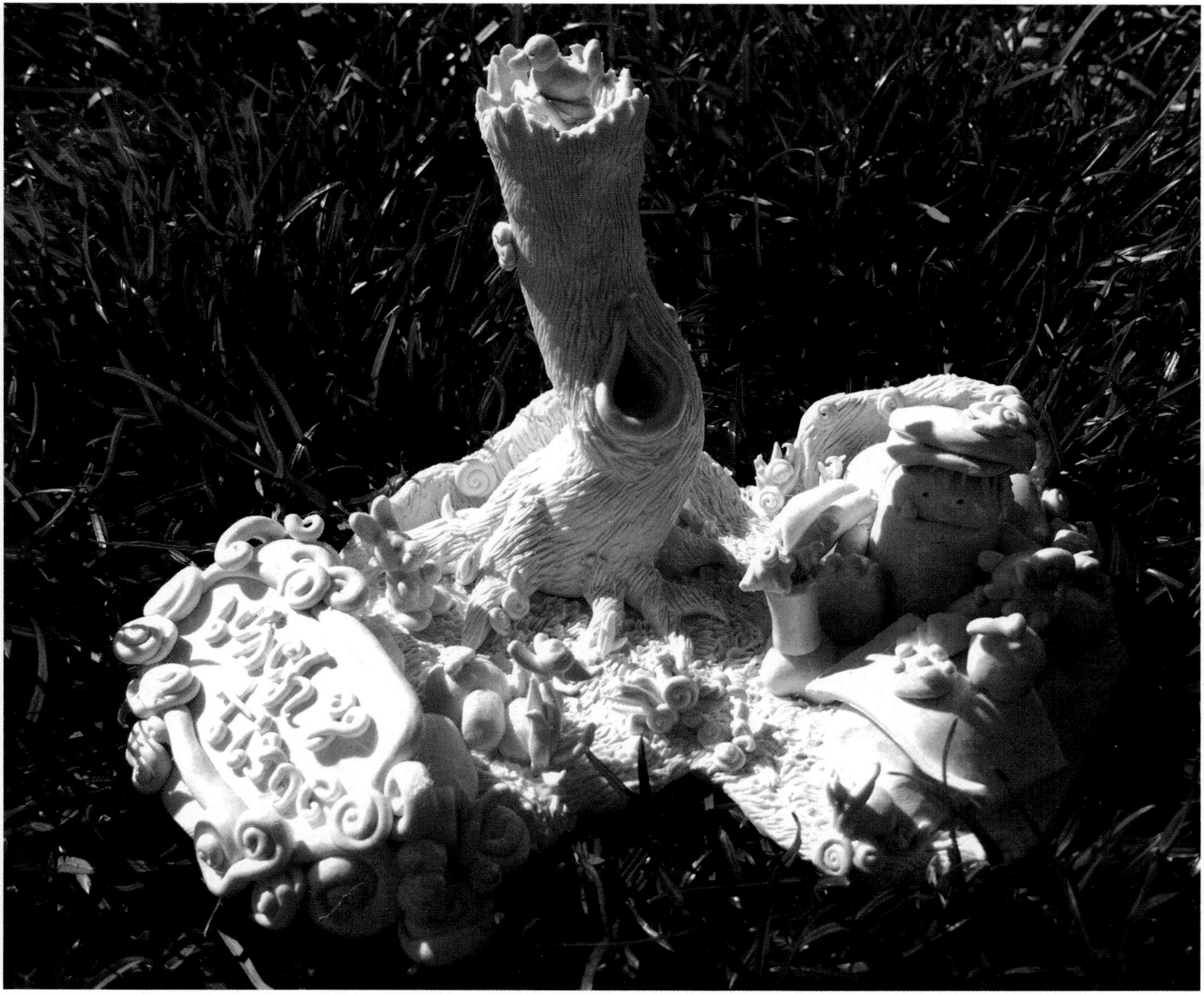

gronk sculptures by katie

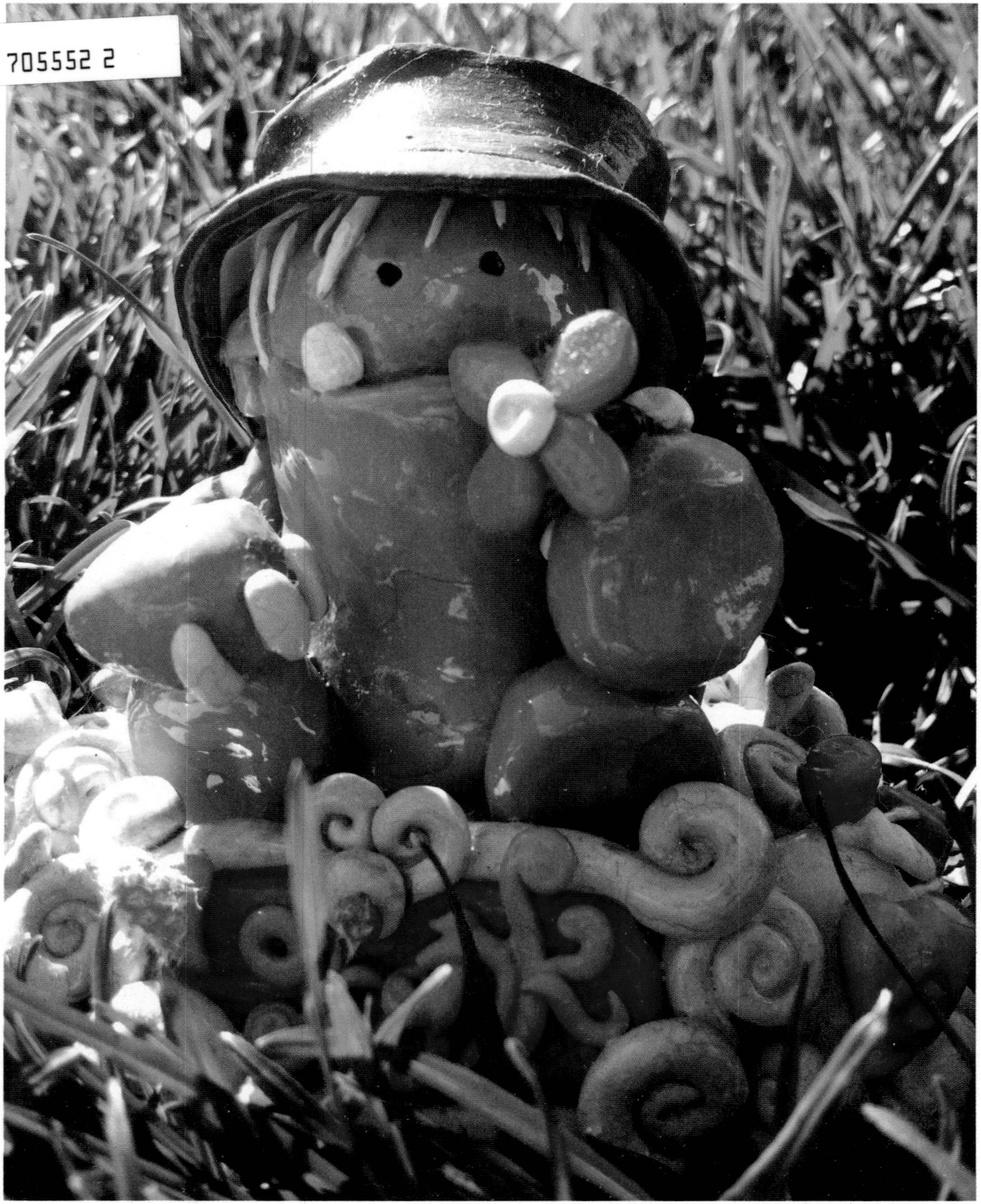